AF088356

James Cooke

Alien Contactee

James Cooke

Alien Contactee

Daniel J Clay

Copyright © 2018 Daniel J. Clay

The moral right of the author has been asserted.

Apart from any fair dealing for the purposes of research or private study, or criticism or review, as permitted under the Copyright, Designs and Patents Act 1988, this publication may only be reproduced, stored or transmitted, in any form or by any means, with the prior permission in writing of the publishers, or in the case of reprographic reproduction in accordance with the terms of licences issued by the Copyright Licensing Agency. Enquiries concerning reproduction outside those terms should be sent to the publishers.

Matador
9 Priory Business Park,
Wistow Road, Kibworth Beauchamp,
Leicestershire. LE8 0RX
Tel: 0116 279 2299
Email: books@troubador.co.uk
Web: www.troubador.co.uk/matador
Twitter: @matadorbooks

ISBN 9781789010053

British Library Cataloguing in Publication Data.
A catalogue record for this book is available from the British Library.

Front & Back cover design: Oliver Clay © 2017

Printed and bound in the UK by 4edge limited
Typeset in 11pt Minion Pro by Troubador Publishing Ltd, Leicester, UK

Matador is an imprint of Troubador Publishing Ltd

Dedicated to my Mum, who died 14 years to the day after James Cooke and who I like to think is somewhere 'beyond the spirit world' having a chuckle about my laughable travails.

contents

	Foreword	ix
	Introduction	xi
1	James Cooke Biographical Information	1
2	A Night to Remember	4
3	The James Cooke Zomdic Experience	18
4	The Swinging 60s	44
5	James Cooke in the Ufological Literature	55
6	Contactees	64
7	Runcorn Window Area	98
8	James Cooke Spiritualist	108
	Bibliography	124
	Thanks and acknowledgments	127

Foreword

On top of Runcorn Hill, at the western edge of the North West industrial town it takes its name from, is a fixed metal compass atop a plinth. It displays the distance to local points of interest. Mount Snowden is 59 miles away, Blackpool Tower 36 miles and Chester Cathedral 11.2 miles. Closer to home the fascinating 11th century Halton Castle is a mere two miles.

One destination not mentioned on this pleasing installation is the Planet Zomdic. Yet a man from the town claimed to have travelled to just such a place from this hill.

I doubt that any Runcornian with even a passing interest in UFOs could have failed to come across the tale of James Cooke, onetime resident of that parish.

Oh yeah, the first alien abductee, who came from Runcorn and after his experience set up an alien cult church in the city and vanished in the 60s – they may say.

But what is really known about this enigmatic character? Having been fascinated by UFOs and the possible existence of intelligent extraterrestrial life since a young age and being brought up in Runcorn, I wanted to present James's tale.

So here it is, let his message weigh softly on your shoulders.

Introduction

The *UFO Encyclopedia* compiled by John Spencer, published by Headline in 1991,[1] an excellent resource for all things ufological, contains a short entry on 'James Cook'. Leaving aside the misspelling of his name, which was actually Cooke, the entry sums up his contribution to and place in the history of ufology in just 11 lines. This is akin to Douglas Adams's wry observation about the Earth, in *The Hitchhiker's Guide to the Galaxy*.[2] The entry for Earth in the guide simply says 'harmless' with guide contributor and galactic traveller Ford Prefect attempting to expand this to 'mostly harmless'.

According to James Cooke, he, like Prefect, was a galactic traveller. Like Earth's entry, his story should be expanded and told in full. The main claims generally understood about this enigmatic and elusive character are:

- In September 1957 he was contacted by aliens telepathically. They put it to James that he should meet them on the top of a hill and accompany them on a journey to their home planet.
- James, clearly an intrepid character, agreed to

---

1 *The UFO Encyclopedia* – John Spencer, Headline, London 1991
2 *The Hitchiker's Guide to the Galaxy* – Douglas Adams, Pan Books, Basingstoke 1979

this, met the aliens on top of Runcorn Hill and travelled with them to a Planet called Zomdic.
- In doing this he secured his place in Ufology as the first alien abductee from Britain and possibly Europe.
- Aside from seeming to simply want to show James around their home world, they also gave him a message to pass to his fellow humans, warning of the dangers posed by both atomic weaponry and ecological devastation.
- James returned to Earth and set up two churches dedicated to his alien-given mission to spread the word about the dangers facing Earth. He continued to communicate with the Zomdickians (*my phrase*) telepathically.
- The churches lasted for around 10 years

And then…well the received wisdom is that the trail goes cold and James vanishes. I hope in this book to provide an analysis of James's tale, a resource to draw on over how the story has been presented and passed along the line of ufological literature and also to address the question of what may have actually happened.

Wikipedia deleted his entry, and the remnants of the debate as to whether he was relevant enough to include are depressing.[3] Here is a man who we will go on to show is a pivotally intriguing figure in the history of outsider thought in the UK.

---

3   https://en.wikipedia.org/wiki/Wikipedia:Articles_for_deletion/James_Cooke_(abductee)

The confidently asserted facts in the discussion about the reason for deletion are plain wrong. "The local paper being the source that seems to have the most information – a single paragraph." – wrong. "Where is the substantial coverage? There is one mention of him in a non-notable newspaper – *The Warrington Guardian*." – wrong! "Claiming you've been abducted by aliens does not make you notable, even if you're the first to do so." – wrong! Whatever you think of alien abduction claims, and clearly a lot of people don't think much of them, being the first person to claim something which is a huge cultural phenomenon, is significant.

There is also a suggestion that the whole thing might be a hoax. Well, I have seen his birth and death certificates, photograph and interviews with him from 1957 and 1958 respectively, so it is conclusively and irrefutably not a hoax.

To be fair to the debaters who agreed to kick him into the Wiki trash can, they were clearly not aware of the first-hand accounts and multiple references in the ufological literature over the decades. They are also in the dark as to what he represents culturally and his value as a lens and thermometer for the state of outsider thought and alternative religions of his time.

The map overleaf shows the key areas of his tale.

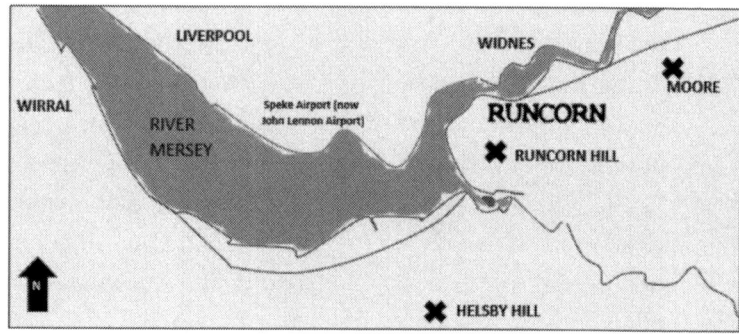

James Cooke's locality.

(Map by Ben Clay.)

one
James Cooke Biographical Information

> Orbiting Earth in the spaceship, I saw how beautiful our planet is. People, let us preserve and increase this beauty, not destroy it
>
> *Yuri Gagarin*

James Cooke was born on 18th December 1908, the youngest of five children.

His father is registered as William Henry Cooke, whose occupation is listed as a waterman. His mother was called Agnes Elizabeth Cooke (nee Hughes) whose occupation is not given, there being no section for female occupations on birth certificates in that era.[1] Being a waterman in Runcorn in 1908 would indicate his father worked on the canals in some capacity. One feature of Runcorn is of course its canals, with the Bridgewater being arguably the most notable, connecting Runcorn, which sits on the Mersey, to both the city of Manchester and the Cheshire town of Leigh.

The registrar of James's birth is one Thomas Cooke but there is no indication if he is any relation to James's family. Either way this future galactic traveller and infamous figure in the history of ufology entered planet Earth in the Registration District of Runcorn and the sub-district of

---

1   Birth certificate obtained by author

Runcorn in the County of Chester. We would say Cheshire today I think or maybe Halton. Runcorn has a complicated sense of identity, but in 1908 Chester was the county name de jour.

The census of 1911, when James was aged two, places the family at 5 Byron Street, Runcorn. As an interesting aside and coincidence, this was the street where two doors down, at number 1 Byron Street, there would be a notorious poltergeist incident in 1952, five years before James would travel to Zomdic[2].

Byron Street is opposite Victoria Road Cemetery in Runcorn, close to Runcorn Old Town Station.

By the time of the 1911 census, James's father William is detailed as a 'barge captain'. This may be an upgrade from his 'waterman' occupation on James's birth certificate or could just be a more detailed description of his day job.

His mother Agnes Elizabeth is noted as a housewife. James had three older sisters, the oldest being Elizabeth aged 13, followed by Eliza aged 11 and Bessie aged six. He also had an elder brother, William Henry who was four years older than him.

The Sunday People in 1966 describes him as a 'former furniture salesman'.[3]

James died on 29th July 1993 aged 84 in Halton General Hospital, Runcorn.[4] For all the galactic escapades of his 40s, in terms of Earth, he had lived and died in the same Cheshire town.

---

2   *Paranormal Merseyside*, SD Tucker, 2013, Amberley publishing, Stroud.

3   *The Sunday People*, 17 July 1966 page 4

4   Death certificate obtained by author

His occupation at the time of his death is given as 'greengrocery manager (retired)' and his place of residence as Churchill Mansions, Runcorn. Like many place names in towns given the moniker 'mansions', there is nothing stately or grandiose about the place. It is Runcorn's only tower block, in the 'Old Town' and within a javelin throw of the Silver Jubilee Bridge. A one-bedroom flat in Churchill Mansions these days will cost you shy of £40,000.[5]

The cause of his death was twofold, bronchopneumonia and cerebrovascular accident. Cerebrovascular accident is a stroke in common parlance and bronchopneumonia acute inflammation of the lungs.

I have had family members in Halton Hospital and it is strange to ponder that James might have been there at the same time I visited them, or I might have walked past him on High Street in the Old Town (as in not the New Town) of Runcorn: a man who ended up as a greengrocery manager, who people passed without a double glance, with no idea that he occupied such a niche place in the history of ufology, one of the major phenomena of the post-Second World War culture.

What stories would he have had? Would he have stuck to his tales of intergalactic journeys or would he have recanted them? What did he make of the fact he was in UFO encyclopaedias and contactee books and on the new-fangled internet?

All of this and he was also a man in a hospital, in his 80s, who lived in a tower block and whose death certificate was witnessed by his older sister Eliza who was herself in her 90s at the time of his death.

---

5   hwww.rightmove.co.uk (correct as of 11th May 2017)

TWO
A NIGHT TO REMEMBER

There are more things in heaven and earth Horatio,
Than are dreamt of in your philosophy
William Shakespeare[6]

Flying Saucer Review (FSR) picked up James's story in 1958[7] and dispatched a Miss Thelma Roberts to spend a whole weekend with him at his home in Runcorn, interviewing him about his story. This was presented as the lead item in their *Recent Contacts and Landing Reports* section of the journal.

One myth that should be dispelled straight away is that James was subject to alien abduction. James went with the aliens willingly and in the main had a fine old time. He did not report any paralysis, unwanted invasive probing, helplessly being levitated towards the craft or time loss. Hypnotic regression was not required to pry disturbing memories of large headed, bug eyed aliens performing surgical or reproductive procedures him.

James was asked telepathically to go to Zomdic by the aliens, who told him to meet them on top of a hill and he went. As far as we can tell from the record, he didn't

---
6   *The Tragedy of Hamlet Prince of Denmark* (Hamlet), William Shakespeare circa 1599-1602
7   *Flying Saucer Review* Volume 4, #4, 1958 ed Le Poer Trench, archive available by order www.fsr.org.uk

even discuss this in advance with his mother, who he lived with in Westfield Road, Runcorn, or anyone else. No, they asked him to go and he unquestioningly went.

James reported that his trip to Zomdic took place at just after 2am on Saturday, 7th September 1957.

7th September 1957

Elvis was just about to take over the number one spot in the hit parade from Lonnie Donegan, his *All Shook Up* replacing the double A-side *Puttin on the Style/Gamblin' Man*.[8]

The most notable event according to Wikipedia about the date is that NBC unveiled an animated version of their 'living colour' peacock logo.[9] Harold Macmillan was Prime Minister, Dwight D Eisenhower was in the White House with Khrushchev his counterpart at the Kremlin. *Around The World in 80 Days* starring David Niven and Shirley Maclaine had won best picture at the Oscars.[10]

The Cold War was in full swing. Four months before James had his unforgettable experience, Britain had detonated its first experimental 'nuclear device' at altitude over Christmas Island in the Pacific.[11]

A month after James's purported trip to Zomdic the Soviet Union would launch the Sputnik satellite, the first human made object to orbit the Earth. This was the starting gun for the Space Race, an era of astronauts and cosmonauts.

---

8   www.ukpopcharts.co.uk
9   https://en.wikipedia.org/wiki/1957
10   www.oscars.org
11   http://news.bbc.co.uk/onthisday/hi/dates/stories/may/15/newsid_2510000/2510335.stm

In the world of science-fiction movies, *Invasion of the Body Snatchers* had been released in 1956. Another '56 release, *Earth vs. the Flying Saucers*, saw trailblazer Ray Harryhausen flexing his visionary muscles, using stop motion animation to create the special effects.[12]

Science Fiction novels were growing in popularity, with luminaries such as Isaac Asimov, Robert Heinlein and Arthur C. Clarke prolific in the era. Asimov's seminal *Foundation Trilogy* had concluded in 1953, with *Second Foundation*[13] and he was releasing at least one novel a year. Heinlein and Clarke were also prolific in the 1950s, inviting readers on frequent journeys to fantastical worlds, with names to conjure with such as Jubbulpore[14] and Diaspar[15]; throughout the space time continuum.

Although Asimov, Clarke and Heinlein would come to be revered as the 'big three' of the Golden Age of Science Fiction[16], their output was a drop in the ocean compared to the overall output of books, films and pulp magazines.

TV was lagging behind somewhat, although Buck Rogers and Flash Gordon both made their US small screen debuts in the 1950s. In Britain, it wouldn't really be until the 1960s that British TV, marshalled by the BBC, would truly latch on to the public appetite for the

---

12 https://en.wikipedia.org/wiki/History_of_science_fiction_films#Post-War_and_1950s
13 *Second Foundation*, Isaac Asimov, 1953, Gnome Press
14 *Citizen of The Galaxy*, Robert Heinlein, 1957, Scribners
15 *The City and The Stars,* Arthur C Clarke, 1956, Frederick Muller
16 https://www.wireclub.com/clubs/books/isaac_asimov_fans/conversations/Toj1CgM8CzfoOEM80

creative goldmine that science fiction had become. That said, *The Quatermass Experiment*[17] had been broadcast in 1953, with its tale of a human crew returning from space, with one unfortunate crew member starting the process of metamorphosis into an alien being.

Images and stories of aliens, space travel and close encounters had taken root in popular culture, springing forth a cornucopia of speculation about extraterrestrial lands and the likely motives and ramifications for Earth of their inhabitants.

From a military perspective, the UFO phenomenon had been officially investigated in the UK since at least 1953.[18] This followed on from a wave of sightings in 1952, with many witnesses being RAF employees. In some instances the UFOs had also been picked up on radar systems. The MOD took the decision that from then onwards, they would investigate the reports.[19]

The idea of British airspace being routinely invaded by unidentified craft would of course have been of concern to the Ministry of Defence (MOD) and the military. Rather than being concerned that the craft were the prelude to an invasion from an alien species, the MOD would have in all likelihood been watching out for spy craft from the Soviet Union. It would not be good news for the allied western countries, which had founded the North Atlantic Treaty Organisation (NATO) in 1949 if the Soviets had craft able to outmanoeuvre their most

---

17   The Quatermass Experiment, Nigel Kneale, BBC July-August 1953
18   *Encounter in Rendlesham Forest*, N Pope, J Burroughs, J Penniston, 2014, Thistle, London
19   Ibid

sophisticated military hardware and invade airspace with impunity.

So there was an official watching brief being kept on the phenomenon by the government and military, despite the usual denials of any interest.

The zeitgeist then in the 1950s saw perceptions and interest in UFOs and the prospect of Earth being visited by alien races, permeate society.

Meanwhile back in Runcorn

Five days after James' excursion to Zomdic had ended, local paper the *Runcorn Weekly News and District Reporter* (hereafter referred to as the 'RWN') featured as its headline, 'Workers Rush to Cash ICI Shares'.[20] Important local news of course. Having grown up in Runcorn I am well aware of the symbiotic relationship between chemical industry and the town.

Sharing the front page was another article about industrial relations, 'Councils Clash at Astmoor', Astmoor being an industrial estate. Directly next to James's fantastical tale was the much earthier headline 'Sewage Now a Grave Problem'.

Construction of the Silver Jubilee 'Runcorn' Bridge', providing a vehicle bridge across the Mersey had commenced on 25th April 1956.[21] By the time of its completion in 1960 it would be the third largest steel

---

20 *Runcorn Weekly News* (RWN) 12th September 1957, available on microfilm at Halton Lea Library, Runcorn
21 https://en.wikipedia.org/wiki/Silver_Jubilee_Bridge

arch span bridge on planet Earth, beaten only in scale by Sydney Harbour Bridge and Bayonne Bridge, New York.[22]

The town had very basic material concerns, industrial relations and construction dominating the local headlines.

In the arena of religion, Methodism had established strong roots and seemingly rivalled Anglicanism in the town.[23] Runcorn Spiritualist Church was already an institution, having been established in 1908, the year of James's birth. According to the website of the Runcorn Spiritualist Church, its building itself had originally been built in 1888 by an evangelical preacher who was also a chemist.[24] The church developed[25] having originally been built by the Primitive Methodists as an offshoot of their Greenway Road chapel. The adjunct church enabled them to carry their mission to the Dukesfield area of the town.

The church itself is aesthetically intriguing, sandwiched in one of the Railway Bridge arches of Ashridge Street. It is well worth a look as a curio. I did contact the church to see if they had any further information on James but did not get a response.

Spiritualism had an established, significant and easily recognisable focal point in the town.

---

22 *The Changing Face of Runcorn*, Dave Thompson, 2004, Sutton Publishing, Stroud
23 Ibid page 24
24 Details on Runcorn Spiritualist Church are from their website www.runcorn-snu.org.uk
25 *The Changing Face of Runcorn*, Ibid page 25

James Cooke, Headline Grabber

On Thursday October 10th 1957 the RWN departed from the ongoing narrative about dialectical materialism in action for an altogether more unworldly tale. Their front page headline read 'Runcorn's Flying Saucer Anticipated the Red Moon: spiritualist insists he was first in outer space'. James's tale had broken.

The RWN would also follow up with a further account of James's tale on page three of the subsequent edition of the paper, released on 17th October 1957, which fleshes out some of the details of the story.

The first paragraph of the October 10th report states, 'A Runcorn man claims to have beaten the Russians into outer space by three weeks. His story is sure to be met locally with an incredulity matched only by the astonishment of western international politicians at Russia's fantastic achievement'. Despite the anticipated incredulity the RWN was happy to devote much of the front and back page to James's gee whiz tale.

These initial RWN reports are the closest first-hand sources to the incident available, being released around a month after James's trip to Zomdic allegedly took place. Not only do they enable him to outline in depth his experience, they also clarify one of the main areas of uncertainty about his story.

The article reveals the experience James had was not some sort of road to Damascus, Saul to Paul conversion[26]. James did not go from a flat start to alien contact to establishing his churches.

---

26 The Bible, Acts 9

It reveals that James was already a member of a spiritualist group known as 'The Aquarian Crusades'. In fact it would be fellow members who he returned to after his two day planet-break on Zomdic. Waiting for him at his home, 8 Westfield Road, were his mother and one Ethel King of 11 Cavendish Street. The paper notes that Mrs King had recently returned from Trinidad where her husband was an oil engineer.

Why the RWN thought that a trip to Trinidad was particularly notable is anyone's guess. Foreign trips were still reasonably exotic and unusual perhaps. Maybe they felt it gave credence to the gravitas and sincerity of the witness testimony, along the lines of – her husband's an engineer in Trinidad don't you know, I doubt very much Mrs King is prone to flights of fancy. In any event, if a trip to Trinidad was newsworthy, then a journey to Planet Zomdic was certainly worth fulsome interrogation. Also present were a Mr and Mrs Hocknell and a Mr E Thomas.

James had brought back his notebook from Zomdic, full of detail about the planet and his journey there. According to the RWN, the spiritualists duly signed the document as being a true account of James's story. Essentially this simply confirms that James had returned from somewhere with a notebook full of tales about an alien world.

What happened and what were James' motives?

We will explore James's motives throughout the course of this book but it is worth briefly outlining the various runners and riders.

James was clearly committed to his branch of spiritualism. His relationship to The Aquarian Crusades is referenced frequently in the story he recounts to the RWN.

In terms of his character, the FSR interview from 1958[27] describes him as 'a sincere and kindly person with an open and receptive mind, devoid of vanity and with a keen sense of humour'. This presents James as a charismatic individual who was able to deliver his tale in a surprisingly down-to-earth way.

James had returned with a truly fantastical tale of the world he had visited, replete with its flying cars, moneyless system and ability to imagine items into existence.

So why did James recount this initial story of travel to an alien world? The main options are:

It actually happened
We will interrogate James's description of his experience on Zomdic later but I would suggest we can rule out it being a full and accurate account of an actual journey to another planet; in the material sense at least. James did not return from his trip with any kind of item from Zomdic to verify his tale. He had a notebook and a story.

For 15 minutes of fame
It is possible that James was simply a fantasist who fancied some press attention and local notoriety.

He had a psychic / psychiatric experience
Alternatively, James may have actually experienced

---

[27] Ibid

something in a mental or psychic sense. He already had a spirit guide named Cha Chu Ka[28] who had brokered the meeting between the Zomdickians and himself. He claims in the RWN article that he had seen plenty of alien craft in the past and with regard to seeing the craft while on top of Runcorn Hill at 1.15am on 7th September he remarks 'I wondered if it was just to my psychic vision or clear for all to see'.

Lynn Picknett speculates in *The Mammoth Book of UFOs* that James may have had an episode of Temporal Lobe Epilepsy.[29]

James was a military black ops agent

For more information on this, see *Chapter 6 – Contactees*.

There is a theory that the military intelligence communities will plant people within the UFO community. These plants will come up with outlandish stories regarding alien contact. These tales are so bizarre that UFO witnesses en masse and the subject in general are regarded as deluded and not worth taking seriously.

In doing this, military intelligence are able to sell a dummy to the public, who in the main disregard *all* reports of UFOS and aliens, believing them *all* to have come from fantasists and weirdoes.

My assessment is that if shadowy government agencies are involved in such psy-ops, then they aren't doing a particularly good job as interest in UFOs appears strong and healthy. That said there is no doubt that the

---

28 *RWN* 10th October 1957
29 *The Mammoth Book of UFOs*, Lynn Picknett, 2001, Constable, London

US military has dabbled in this type of thing and I would highly recommend the excellent *Mirage Men* for an exposé of this activity.[30]

Could James have been such a sponsored mole? Well, there is absolutely nothing to link James to the military but of course one would expect that to be the case if this was some sort of beyond top secret misinformation programme.

It is also possible that James had been selected by the intelligence communities as being particularly susceptible to this type of thing and he was subjected to mental manipulation to make him believe he had been in contact with extraterrestrials. His stories did achieve national notoriety and were widely discredited and dismissed. James could feasibly have been an unwitting pawn, used to keep the public eye away from the situation of Earth's airspace being regularly invaded by unknown craft, or from military black ops programmes.

James was intoxicated or on drugs

I'm hesitant to even mention this, the laziest of all debunker theories about people who have experienced phenomenon which can't instantly be replicated on multiple occasions under 'laboratory conditions'. However, it is a theory trotted out whenever someone sees something unidentified. 'Oh they must have had a few drinks' spews forth the theory as though the alcohol on sale in Britain is some sort of extreme peyote or ayahuasca extract.

People drink and take other substances without

---

30 *Mirage Men*, Mark Pilkington, 2010 Constable, London also the documentary based on the book 'Mirage Men', 2013, Dir: John Lundberg & Roland Denning

instantly believing they have travelled to another world and bobbed around that world in musically-powered hover cars.

James may have been regularly out of his mind on industrial strength hallucinogens but there is absolutely no indication of this, even when later in the 1960s the British tabloids would briefly and sneerily turn their attention to his activities and tales.

An irresistible unconscious desire from the collective subconscious

This idea will be explored in greater depth in *Chapter 6 – Contactees*. It is a theory proposed by one of the founding fathers of psychoanalysis, Carl Jung. Jung postulated that the saucers being seen where a materialisation of a subconscious symbol of a circle, representing the desire to heal the rift and fractures within the human psyche and also between the human psyche and the divine.

It is a hypothesis which is more or less impossible to refute and impossible to prove, short of somehow uncovering records of James's having spent time on the psychiatrist's couch. The notion of a collective unconscious is an intriguing theory but a speculative theory for all of that. Jung would argue that the saucers rather than coming from outer space, in fact came from inner space, being perceived as no less real to the experiencer.

To promote and progress The Aquarian Crusades

We are moving further into the arena of speculation here of course. James's motives and what actually happened are unknowable. However a clue can perhaps be found in another headline on the back page of the 10th October edition of the RWN below his story, which states 'Church Requires New Members and Money' in relation to the established mainstream Christian church.

James presented his story to the local press very much within the context of him being part of The Aquarian Crusades spiritualist group.

Given that James is so free with his discussions of the Aquarian Crusades and they are happy to sign his notebook to rubber stamp his tale, it is clear they approved of the story. Not only that, but the RWN explain that the document, i.e. the notebook, had been produced by the Aquarian Crusades group in conjunction with Mr Cooke. Note that the document was produced by the group with Mr Cooke. This was an official release to the press and wider society by The Aquarian Crusades.

This is fascinating as it provides the most likely motive for James's desire to promote his story, despite his protestations that 'almost as much as the journey, I dread the telling on my return, to be disbelieved is often the payment all true seekers have to pay for conveying the truth'.

James's tale of his experiences on Zomdic read like a pulp science fiction tale. However, he weaves the experience into the tapestry of his commitment to his brand of spiritualism. In doing this, James is updating the positioning of the Aquarian Crusades and their offer, for the sci-fi age. The mainstream Christian church were making a plea for members and financial support. James's group, in linking spiritualism to alien contact and obtaining local headline coverage were doing an impressive job of getting their group name out there and offering something new.

What will become absolutely clear when we investigate James's account of his extraordinary journey to Zomdic in the next chapter is that he fits into the contactee tradition, established in the United States earlier on in the decade by, among others, George Adamski.

Much like the magnificent steel arch span bridge being constructed across the Mersey linking Cheshire to Merseyside, James himself was a bridge: a bridge between Victorian spiritualism and the Space Age, a bridge between the alien contactee movement in the United States and Europe, a bridge between the pre-atomic and atomic age, a bridge between the industrial revolution and environmental concerns and according to James's own account, a bridge between planet Earth and Zomdic.

Three
The James Cooke Zomdic Experience

> Anything one man can imagine,
> other men can make real.
> *Jules Verne – Around the World in 80 Days*[31]

The RWN articles from October 1957 together with the FSR interview, issue 4 volume 4 from 1958, constitute James's own first-hand account of his trip to Zomdic. In this chapter, I will examine exactly what James had to say.

In the RWN, the story James outlines actually began 20 years prior in 1937. During a séance, James's mother was informed that James was a 'Chosen One'. James then spins his tale forwards 20 years without further elucidation on this revelation.

James advises he was told of the approaching opportunity to travel to another planet and in the quietness of his sanctuary he was informed of the approximate time and place. James says 'I even doubted the mechanism by which the message had been delivered, thinking 'wish may be father to the thought".

He proceeds to outline that one night, he had received more complete instructions, which appear to

---
31 *Around the World in Eighty Days,* Jules Verne, 1873 (various but author's copy: Dean & Son, London)

have come to him via a variant of automatic writing, automatic typing. Sitting by his bed, James typed out the messages coming from his alien interlocutors. 'Be Ready…Be prepared…Bring a sharp instrument' being the rather blunt instructions. The instruction to bring a sharp instrument is a truly unexpected request from a race which has mastered intergalactic travel. Why such a species would not be in possession of or be able to provide a sharp instrument is completely inexplicable. The request is also quite vague, no guidelines being given on size for example. Even if such an alien race had no call for sharp instruments or they were outlawed, one would think they could fashion an appropriate tool. The instruction is more in line with people going on a trip and asking one of the party to bring a travel iron. In attempting to make his story sound plausible and matter of fact, James has in fact left a huge question mark hovering over its already slender credulity.

In addition, to tell James to 'Be ready! Be Prepared!' seems woefully lacking in practical detail. Given that astronauts will have intensive and lengthy training programmes for even the most basic journeys into space, just telling a previously Earthbound human to 'be ready' seems somewhat remiss.

James explains that at 1am on Saturday, September 7th 1957, he saw the pre-arranged symbol quite clearly and with understandable trepidation, ventured out into the cold night. James does not elaborate on the symbol and how or where he saw it. Was it an actual sign or something he viewed through his 'psychic vision'? Alas, we are unlikely ever to know.

James took himself to the appointed place, taking position there at 1.15am. It was at 1.30am that the alien craft revealed themselves, flying in formation, James noting that 'they twist, turn, hover and shoot in interesting, varying acrobatics'.[32] After this display the craft vanished at high speed disappearing beyond the horizon.

There is of course a chance that James has happened upon some sort of aerial phenomenon, although he does not describe the weather as being stormy or electrically charged. Possibly he has seen a meteor shower. The description he offers sounds like a Red Arrows display. Aerial acrobatic displays had been ongoing since the 1920s. According to Wikipedia the first official RAF display team, formed by No. 111 Squadron, came into effect in 1956[33], although there is no mention of this on the RAF historical timeline.[34] The RAF was unlikely to perform an impromptu display in the middle of the night of course and I only mention aerial display here as the description James gives is probably based on knowledge of such displays, which were popular at the time.

Also worth considering is why the aliens would want to treat James to such a display. It didn't appear to serve any purpose other than to illustrate the fantastical nature of their craft. Just aliens showing off. James says it was 2.07am before they returned. He had been on the verge of calling it a night, remarking somewhat nonchalantly that he had seen similar sights on a number of previous

---

32 *RWN* ibid
33 https://en.wikipedia.org/wiki/Red_Arrows#History
34 http://www.raf.mod.uk/history/rafhistorytimeline195059.cfm

occasions, just 'not by arrangement'. He notes, 'on two other occasions I have seen the ships at close quarters. On one of these I was only a matter of 30 yards or so away because I have seen them fairly often'. Despite this previous exposure, he talks of the courage required to venture onto the craft, when eventually the opportunity arose.

James harkens back to his status as a 'Chosen One' when he remarks on his edginess about coming back to Earth and reporting on his experiences. He says, 'luckily, the results of disbelief have changed with the ages for had I had this experience but one or two hundred years ago the disbelief in those days had a penalty attached thereto, a rather painful way of leaving this world of flesh for the world of the spirit'. This seems both highly melodramatic and a rather blunt attempt by James to liken himself to religious martyrs. It also reveals James as a somewhat verbose and erudite individual.

The inference is that if he had told his tale of alien contact a century or two earlier, he would have been killed for his beliefs. In fairness the histories of most major religions are not synonymous with tolerance of tales which contradict their own paradigms. His tale of alien higher intelligence may have found him at odds with The Spanish Inquisition or other religious enforcers.

His next statement, although seemingly elusive and nonsensical, I believe provides the sharp object we need to surgically slice through the opaque flesh of his motives. 'In these writings I do not wish to infer I have been to, and speak of, the Spirit World just beyond this mortal world of flesh. The experience of which I write is beyond the spirit world'. The comment makes little sense. Surely an actual alien world could not be considered beyond the spirit world. However, James is again, albeit ham-fistedly, attempting to link his experiences to spiritualism. His presentation of extraterrestrial contact is something he wants to be considered in tandem with the spirit world and not a threat to spiritualism. He is attempting to update his spiritualist belief system for the age of humanity's journey into space.

An important character in the tale is then referenced by James, his spirit guide Cha-chu-ka. Cha-chu-ka, appears via a projection through the craft's side. Why Cha-chu-ka appears by projection is unclear but adds to the sense of advanced technology. Cha-chu-ka reassures the nervous James, who is by this stage getting cold feet and considering making a run for it, motioning him over to the craft, which tilts to accommodate his forthcoming boarding.

A force freezes James to the spot while he is on one leg and he is unable to move momentarily. This is for his benefit as the alien occupants have a warning message for him. A glowing light shone on his head 'as though from all directions at once' with a voice inside him advising 'jump, do not step, jump on to this stair. The ground is damp. Jump. Don't have one foot on the step and the other on the ground or you will be hurt'.

A flight of stairs numbering 17 or 18 steps appears and James, complying with the Zomdickian's instructions jumps two, from where he easily enters the craft via a 'funnel'. This all sounds Earthly in the extreme. Stairs and a warning akin to a 'mind the gap' station announcement are not what you would expect from an inter-galactic travelling intelligent species.

In James's interview with FSR in 1958[35] he elaborates on what happened once he had entered the craft, saying that the voice which had told him to jump also wanted him to remove his clothing. Fortunately for James this wasn't the prelude to some good old grey alien probing or enforced coupling with a growling female alien, along the lines of what Brazilian farmer Antonio Villas Boas would report just over a month later.[36]

In fact the Zomdickians had provided an alien jumpsuit for him. James describes how he had to stretch it on, putting his legs in first, followed by arms and hands. He then pulled on the head part and mask, noting that the mask lips were sealed together, begging the question of what point they served. The suit was joined at the front waist to points over each hip and when James had put on the head and face he was told to fasten up at the back, just by bringing the fabric together. Having done this the suit sealed itself as it touched. This sounds a bit like Velcro but James describes the suit as being made from a 'plastic-like' material which he says is 'far superior…to anything on this planet'.

He is also provided with shoes which he describes as having 'a peculiar design on them at the bottom'.[37] They are made from the same plastic substance and the soles and uppers are a single form as though from one mould. James is able to stretch them on and finds them 'firm and comfortable'.

---

35 *FSR* vol 4, issue 4, 1958 ibid
36 *The UFO Encyclopedia*, John Spencer ibid pages 47-48
37 *RWN* 10th Oct 1957

His description reminded me somewhat of the Action Man space suit I had as a child. An all in one suit, almost impossible to get over Action Man without copious amounts of talc. Despite his difficulties, James was able to don the plastic type apparel without talc or lotions of any kind.

The interior of the craft is described as 'massive looking with a very large floor area'.[38] He says that 'the light comes from everywhere and no shadow is cast'. Despite the decidedly non-futuristic method of hopping onto a flight of stairs to enter the craft, the steps do have the ability to disappear 'mysteriously'. In place of the steps is a smooth metal wall, 'curved like the inside of a funnel'.

So James finds himself inside a huge funnel shaped craft, equipped and ready with his sharp object.

His notebook scribblings switch to present tense stating, 'I have been writing this while waiting to see the outcome of my entry to this room, but nothing seems to be happening except a slight tremor now and again. I have begun to feel a little drowsy and find difficulty in co-ordinating mind and movement'.

James doesn't report any weightlessness directly, although he does mention later in his account that he was strapped down for periods of time while he slept. He doesn't mention nausea either, a common symptom for humans travelling into space so presumably the craft was advanced enough to replicate Earth's gravitational environment somewhat.

Difficulties with co-ordination are experienced by humans when travelling into space. NASA advises that

---

38 *RWN*, 10th October 1957

in space a person's sense of up and down becomes mixed up, as the vestibular system (this is the apparatus of the inner ear responsible for balance) can't figure out which way is up or down.[39] However this is supposedly due to weightlessness, which James doesn't report. He is only strapped down during sleep.

The human proprioceptive system is also disrupted when travelling in space. This is 'the process by which the body can vary muscle contraction in immediate response to incoming information regarding external forces, by utilizing stretch receptors in the muscles to keep track of the joint position in the body'.[40]

So while travelling through space, James could well expect to have problems with his co-ordination and perhaps the aliens had induced drowsiness in him by way of sedation.

His next notebook entry is timed at 3.20am, with James noting that while he was asleep he saw his body in the same way he did when in a 'trance state'. He was strapped to a table-like shelf projecting from inside of the wall of the ship. Again this talk of being in 'trance state' is significant as a state of being that any self-respecting spiritualist would be familiar with. With James referring to viewing himself from outside of his body, it would appear that he experiences or claims to experience astral projection. It also hints at the possibility that James may have experienced the whole Zomdic journey as a form of lucid dream.

He notes his thoughts are picked up by an unseen force

---

39 http://www.space.com/23017-weightlessness.html
40 http://www.spdaustralia.com.au/the-proprioceptive-system/

and his wants anticipated, mental telepathy continuing to be the communication tool of choice. Again, James is blending together the usual ingredients of mesmerism with science fiction to create a new para-spiritual-science-fictional smoothie.

James goes on to describe in quite convoluted fashion how he would walk around the ship but when he felt tired would go to sleep. He says he has no memory of his body being strapped down on the table, which presumably happens when he falls asleep. He speaks of a main room which is entered via a telepathically operated door, with 'no handle, no hinges, no jambs'.

He says of his sleepy travelling experience that even though he didn't see anyone in the initial ship he entered, this doesn't necessarily mean that no other being was there as he later learned the world to which he travelled was one of 'thought language'. His interpretation of how he can open the door using his mind, is that his thought that he wishes to open the door is picked up by the Zomdic telepaths who then use their telekinetic ability to open the door for him.

The stairs of the ship eventually reappeared and James was told to descend from the ship to a larger one. Editor of FSR in 1958, Brinsley Le Poer Trench, the 8th Earl of Clancarty, notes 'presumably he was now on a mothership'.[41] It is Cha-chu-ka who has motioned for James to descend to the mothership.[42]

Eventually James arrived at the mothership. To disembark from the craft he left Earth on, he says the part

---

41   *FSR* vol 4, no 4 ibid
42   *RWN* 10th Oct 1957 ibid

nearest to him lifted into the air while the part furthest away remained at the same level, to reveal the entrance to the mothership. This gave him the sensation of walking into a huge monstrous cavern, a huge mouth waiting to swallow him. He notes that his first step was tinged with 'bravado'.[43] This was a small but brave step for a human from Runcorn and a potentially giant leap for Runcornkind.

James Cooke was soon to arrive on Zomdic.

The Mothership

In James's interview with FSR he mentions that there were well over 20 people on the large ship which Le Poer Trench believed to be the mothership. From this we can conclude that his journey to the mothership probably happened after travelling almost all the way to Zomdic in the smaller ship. James will confirm this in his account, outlining that there are saucer-shaped ships that operate in the surroundings of the planet the travellers from Zomdic are visiting. They themselves have larger ships waiting elsewhere in the wider cosmos.

His first meeting with the beings on the mothership is intriguing. James recalls clearly the expressions on the faces of the meet and greet aliens, who for telepaths had quite a visual method of greeting him, first placing their left hands over their eyes, followed by then placing their right hands over their hearts. He notes that the aliens could read his every thought and that he only had to think something and the thought would be answered. He also

---

43   *RWN* 10th Oct 1957 ibid

outlines that this made it impossible to deceive as you couldn't say one thing while meaning another.[44] I would imagine ubiquitous telepathy may pose problems for the duplicitous, conniving, psychologically confused human race but James is not critical.

James says the beings were tall by Earth standards but he would learn small by Zomdic standards.[45] He puts their height at somewhere between 6ft 6ins and 6ft 9ins. Perhaps there was some advantage to having smaller members of their race as the off planet mothership team, taking up less space and less weight.

James tries to move towards them but feels as though he is carrying a great weight.[46] The inference here presumably is that James was struggling to adjust to the gravitational conditions on the mothership. Alternatively, the Zomdickians may have utilised some sort of force to prevent James from moving towards them, hedging their bets, perhaps fearful that a human being tooled up with a 'sharp implement' presented with such a situation would revert to type and attack them.

A voice (I think Cha-chu-ka's based on his account, although he doesn't specify) says 'they wish wholesome sights to bring you happiness'. James muses on how kind the Zomdickians look, who are standing around smiling at him.[47]

In this mothership reception room is a seat set in front of a table with an umbrella-shaped cover over it. There is

---

44 *FSR* ibid
45 *RWN* 10th Oct 1957 ibid
46 *RWN* 10th Oct 57
47 *RWN* 10th Oct 57

a rod in the centre of the table supporting a whole load of wires (although James isn't totally sure they are wires, noting 'if wires they were'). This does sound somewhat like a modern computer server room.

On the whole though, the mothership room is much like the room on the initial craft aside from it being straight edged rather than curved.

In any event, the aliens take James to Planet Zomdic, telling James 'your scientists don't know this planet exists'. James tactfully doesn't ask the Zomdickians why they don't just go and tell Earth's scientists of their existence. To give the benefit of the doubt, if the aliens can only communicate with particularly psychically sensitive humans to convey their 'world of thought language', then there may not have been a 'chosen one' among the scientific community, who fit the bill.

Planet Zomdic

The first thing James outlines in his interview with FSR relates to the transport system on the planet. Although there are roads, these are regarded by the Zomdickians as antiquated and are not in use. Instead they utilise small hover ships that travel around some 20 to 30 feet in the air.

These small ships apparently operated on a kind of musical harmonic principle. The pilot would sit in a bucket-shaped seat in front of a table. Using a small object like a hammer, the pilot would tap on a row of metal-like strips which protruded like organ stops. Melodious 'ping' noises would sound with the note sounding at one level for a while before rising higher and higher.

Teasing out what James is describing, it sounds as though the higher the note, the higher the altitude of the craft. Quite a neat concept.

In flight James comments that the hover ships were controlled by a small ball, which the pilot operated via his left hand. So in place of a steering wheel, the Zomdickian flying craft have a ball, which sounds something akin to the way one navigates with a modern day computer mouse.

So we have a craft whose altitude is controlled in accordance with the pitch of a musical note (or perhaps this was just an electronic feature of the craft feeding back to the pilot how high it was) and direction controlled by a mouse like ball.

Even on landing the musical sounds continued until the pilot took their hand away from the steering ball. The pilot was then required to use their hammer to knock down 'certain strips' which caused the humming to cease and for everything to be still.

A visual image of how such a musical extra-terrestrial craft might look can be seen in a 2017 episode of BBC children's programme The Clangers[48].

In terms of Zomdic's flora, the vegetation predominantly consists of small yellow herbs with blue tipped leaves. James refers to Zomdic's flowers as 'superb' but sadly doesn't elaborate further. The herbs sound something like our Earth's Tansy (Tanceteum Vulgare).[49]

---

48 The Clangers 'The Sound Snatcher' CBeebies, first broadcast 12th September 2017
49 https://wildseed.co.uk/species/view/264

Having wowed James with their superb flowers and Space Tansy the Zomdickians follow this up by taking him to meet one of their 'wise men' for a lecture on the importance of the balance of nature.

The environment was certainly becoming an increasingly important issue in 1950s Britain. The first Clean Air Act came into force in 1956, largely as a response to the Great London Smog of December 1952, which had lasted for the best part of a week, killing thousands.[50]

'Listen,' the wise man said to James. It is a bit unexpected that the wise man had to try and get James' attention, although to be fair he may at this point have been looking around distractedly at the flying musical ships and stunning floral arrangements. Having got his attention, the Zomdickian wise man continued, 'The inhabitants of your planet will upset the balance, if they persist in using force instead of harmony. Warn them of the danger.'

Incidentally, I am using the gender specific term 'wise man' advisedly as this is how James refers to him. He will also tell Thema Roberts that the people on Zomdic are 'bi-sexual'. By this I assume he means asexual or hermaphroditic rather than having the advantage of immediately being able to double their chances of a date on Saturday night, as Woody Allen once quipped.

In his account to the RWN, James says 'the force or power we seek on Earth is based on True Harmony. This power has material as well as spiritual uses and should not be left unused. From the study based on harmonics we can

---

50 http://www.air-quality.org.uk/03.php

find many answers to questions that have baffled many of the 'great' minds of old'.[51]

This all sounds very portentous but unfortunately is completely lacking in any kind of practical advice on how to apply or harness True Harmony to resolve the unresolved questions which James alludes to.

The beings on Zomdic have adopted the classic sci-fi dress code of wearing two piece garments with a belted waist. Their faces are baby-faced although some do have beards, which you would think might indicate some sort of gender diversity being in place but this is not expanded on.

There is no system of money on Zomdic, the inhabitants simply having what they need with the ability to turn energy into anything they like. A moneyless society of course does not seem particularly surprising in the early part of the 21st century with our credit cards, online banking and bitcoins. Likewise the fact that everything consists of energy is not a hugely mind-blowing concept now, with increased understanding of what happens at an atomic level and the rise of quantum physics theory. What James is being told here is ahead of its time and this does indicate some sort of scientific theory being imparted to him which would be relatively unknown in 1957; certainly in terms of the working knowledge of the general populace.

It should be considered though, that the likes of Max Planck, Niels Bohr and Albert Einstein had pioneered ideas and theories with regard to atomic science. James as a clearly inquisitive and open minded individual, well may

---

51 *RWN* 17th Oct 1957 ibid

have come across and pondered on such theories and their potential ramifications.

Having been taken all the way to Zomdic to be given a rather basic message about the possible pitfalls of not living harmoniously with nature and the dangers of war, James makes the reasonable point 'but they won't listen to me'. You can imagine him thinking 'but they might listen to you if instead of appearing over Runcorn Hill in the middle of the night, you put on your spectacular aerobatic displays over the Whitehouse, the Kremlin or Trafalgar Square on a bank holiday' but James stoically keeps such thoughts to himself.

I do not want to sound snarkily sarcastic about James's tale at this point, after all he himself has blurred the boundaries about whether this is a material planet or something of a more psychic nature. His experience may be more akin to a vision and these have been taken entirely seriously by large swathes of humanity even when, in fact particularly when, relating to ancient seers and prophets. One person's life-changing prophecy is another person's gateway to ridicule. For example, most of us are familiar with the story of a man who had messages of peace, harmony and other teachings for humankind based on messages from higher intelligence, these messages being taken to heart by his followers but rejected and held up to ridicule and hostility by others of his time. Yes, I am talking of Erich von Däniken.[52]

This is James's own tale of a higher intelligence imploring mankind to live in peace and harmony with

---

52   Check out www.daniken.com/en/

each other and nature. Sixty years later James, I'm listening, even if no-one else is or has.

The wise man is sympathetic. In response to James saying that humanity will not listen to him, he sighs 'or anyone else either'. James is told about the method of propulsion through space, although this is not elaborated on.

The wise man does clarify that motherships are used in outer space and saucers are used as some sort of propelling force utilising the magnetic fields surrounding the Earth or whichever planet they are visiting. The saucers 'tune in' to both the planet and the person they wish to contact.

This explanation of how the Zomdickians travel across the vast distances of deep space is given to James by way of 'mental pictures'. Apparently James also received further revelations from his alien hosts but he says 'of the other things I must, for the time being, remain silent'.[53]

The alien hospitality does extend to food. James had not eaten since the Friday night before his journey and he felt very thirsty. Merely thinking that he was hungry and thirsty resulted in a tumbler shaped, semi-transparent, slightly pliable container appearing. This sounds very much like a Tupperware beaker. This beaker was full of a white substance, tasting like coconut milk but much richer in consistency, with a 'bitter-sweet tang'.[54] The substance satiates both his thirst and his hunger.

Having imparted their message to James and shown him around a bit, the Zomdickians give him a lift back to Earth.

---

53 *RWN* 17th Oct 1957
54 *RWN* ibid

Return to Runcorn

Aside from having difficulties in extricating himself from his plastic suit, the journey home appears to have gone smoothly. James says he used a razor blade to get himself out of the alien space garb. He explains the aliens had foreseen this difficulty, hence them telling him he might want to come with a blade. Again this is a Frankenstein combination of the prosaic and the fantastical. James is on an inter-galactic craft after all, yet the civilisation in question who have developed the craft have had to ask him to bring a blade to cut his way out of the spacesuit they provided.

Another point of interest is that the craft James returns to Earth in is the same one that he had travelled to Zomdic in previously. James notes that he retrieved the blade from his coat pocket, which he had left in an untidy pile on the floor of the saucer and which was still there.[55]

We also get an insight into Zomdickian toiletry products. James hasn't been able to check his watch during his time on Zomdic as it is covered up by the space suit. Once freed from the suit he is able to check the time. The time is 5.37am and he judges it to be Sunday morning. After a well-earned nap, James wakes up at 8.50am feeling refreshed and desiring a wash.

In the wall of the craft is 'what looked like a fire extinguisher'.[56] This sounds somewhat like a modern day soap dispenser. Although a version of soap dispensers had been used in medical establishments since the early

---

55 *RWN* 17th Oct 1957
56 *RWN* ibid

19th century, liquid soap itself had not been patented until 1865. In fact it wouldn't be until 1980 that they were introduced into the domestic market by the Minnetoka Corporation.[57]

James is momentarily baffled by the dispenser, but fortunately 'the voice' (presumably Cha-chu-ka) is on hand to instruct him what to do. James takes the creamy substance and washes his hands. He is about to make the dreadful error of washing his face with the same liquid but is reprimanded by 'the voice', which barks 'use the other cream – that one destroys hair!' The whole scene of James being instructed by a disembodied voice in what to do, brings to mind the film Airplane, with the sharp airport public address system announcements to Captain Oveur, telling him which phone he should pick up. Oveur is told to pick up the white phone, reaches for the red, with the voice tersely saying 'no, the white phone'.[58]

His account here is, in truth, full of holes. He explains that the liquid he had used for his hand washing disappears to be replaced by another one for his face. Leaving aside that he now presumably has hairless and perfectly smooth hands, he also says he used the previous cream, which he said had vanished, to remove his beard. In the same description he says it was a good job he didn't use the initial hair-removing cream as he would have been left with no eyebrows.[59]

Perhaps the inference is that the competing creams appeared and disappeared at different times. However,

---

57 http://tenrandomfacts.com/soap-dispenser/
58 Airplane, 1980, Dir: Jim Abrahams, David Zucke
59 *RWN* ibid

the question is begged as to why such an advanced race was unable to develop hand and face creams that weren't dangerously corrosive.

He also gains some insight into why he keeps sleeping and feeling dizzy on the saucer, as opposed to the relative stability of the mothership. James is informed that his sleep was caused by 'deceleration'.[60] Medically speaking, sleep and dizziness could theoretically be caused by rapid deceleration. Intuitively, one can imagine that such changes in momentum would cause a reaction, notably nausea. In terms of sleep inducement and dizziness, this seems to be mainly associated with effects on the brain, for example due to concussion.[61]

Disappointingly James does not return with a sample of space tansy, a photograph of the musical organ ships or a strip of the fabric from his cocoon like Zomdickian space suit. He does though have his notebook.

In the RWN article of 10th October 1957,[62] James says he was returned to Widnes. To say the least, this seems a little odd. Why having travelled through space-time, the Zomdickians would not drop him back in his home town or where they picked him up from is inexplicable. Instead they drop him in neighbouring chemical town Widnes, across the river, meaning he would have faced the inconvenience of utilising the Runcorn Transporter bridge or taken a ferry or a train to cross over the Mersey to get home. The Silver Jubilee Bridge would not be completed until 1961.

---

60   *RWN* 10th Oct 1957
61   www.ncbi.nlm.nih.gov/pmc/articles/PMC4760657/
62   *RWN* 10th Oct 1957

I think here James is again guilty of trying to make his outlandish tale sound matter of fact and thereby giving it more credence but in fact achieving the opposite, with his matter of fact 'yeah they actually would only drop me in Widnes' type remark; as though he had just been on a long car journey with someone who rather than drop him at his door had left him at a junction so they didn't have to go too far or too inconveniently out of their way.

James does provide something approaching an explanation as to why he was returned to Widnes and not closer to his home, or back on top of Runcorn Hill from whence he had departed for Zomdic. He says the Zomdickians explained that the area he had been collected from was being 'scanned' too heavily[63], implying that some sort of military or official reconnaissance was being carried out at the launch site.

Elsewhere in the ufological literature (see later chapter *James Cooke in the Ufological Literature* for references), it is reported that he was returned to Runcorn Hill. In his own account he is returned to Widnes.

Apart from undressing from the Zomdickian spacesuit, the only issue James has is burning his hand on the rail of the spacecraft's stairs when exiting the ship. Mr E. Thomas readily attests he saw the burns on the back of his hand.[64]

James explains that when he left the saucer he burned his hand on the stair rails as he didn't let go of the rail before his feet touched the ground. This led to an electrical current sparking on his hand resulting in the two burn

---

63 *RWN* 11th Oct 1957
64 FSR, vol 4, issue 4, 1958 ibid

scars. The saucer itself does not actually touch the ground at any time, instead hovering just above it.[65]

Hurrying away from underneath the saucer and the cinders its presence has left, James turns to look at the craft once more. With a neat bit of showmanship, the saucer dips 'in salute' then speeds away.

James makes his way home from Widnes, timing his return as 10.50pm on Sunday September 8th 1957. He explains that his mother and his fellow Aquarians had been aware of the offer which had been proffered to James by Chu-cha-ka to travel to an alien world but had not been aware when it would be. He ends his tale 'any of the witnesses to my arrival at home are prepared to confirm about my appearance and mannerisms'.[66]

That then was James' first-hand account of his experience, laid out just over a month on from it. Immediately below his tale is a report on a parking violation, with the headline 'Crossing Was Obscured', a driver making waves for having parked in a prohibited space by a pedestrian crossing. "I have only been to the shops across the way, there is plenty of room for cars to pass." This excuse didn't wash with officialdom and the motorist was fined 10s. Below this tale is another story of a traffic violation, a Widnes man in this instance, fined 10s for failing to stop at a halt sign, "I slowed down," being the flimsy excuse offered.[67] It's a halt sign, not a slow down sign!

Switching from the fantastical swooshings of James's tale of intergalactic contact and travel to the mundanity

---

65 *RWN* 11th Oct 1957
66 *RWN* 11th Oct 1957
67 *RWN* ibid

of parking offences induces the feeling, familiar to all fans of paranormal tales, of a crashing of the senses. The feeling one has when a particularly exciting film ends and the credits roll. We are back here on Earth with motorists paying fines for minor traffic violations. Whatever people think of James and his tale, it does provide colour and fuel for the imagination.

One side bit of insight gleaned from looking at these papers from October 1957, completely unrelated to James, regards Christmas. "Christmas starts too early these days," people bemoan. "In my day we put the tree up on Christmas Eve, the shops now are on it from the middle of October if not earlier, in my day the shops didn't mention Christmas until given express permission by the reigning monarch on 21st December," they continue to spit and gibber. Not so. The RWN issues in October 1957 already had adverts for Christmas shopping trips into Liverpool, pantomimes and the Grotto at Lewis's, with Father Christmas due to arrive (from Zomdic possibly) on 1st November.

There are a number of intriguing headlines from the RWN at this time. Including the misfiring prophecy 'the demand for scientists will not last forever'[68], which on closer inspection turns out to be a veiled threat from local chemical industry bigwigs that scientific employees needn't think they can spend their time slacking off.

There is also another off-target prophetic headline, namely 'there will be a world war sooner than later unless nations 'get together'.'[69]

---

68 *RWN* 31st Oct 1957
69 *RWN* 24th Oct 1957

James is back baby!

James would pop up again in the pages of FSR, two years later in 1960.[70] The story is a re-hashed version of his Zomdic travelogue. November 1959 is given as the date of James next inter-galactic jolly.

Describing James as an 'engineer', this time he is picked up by an E.T. from Helsby Hill, Cheshire and taken to a planet called 'Shebic'. James says the planet is 'bigger' than the Earth, which doesn't exactly help attempt to pinpoint which astronomical body it might be.

The days are longer than Earth's and the nights colder. The inhabitants are a surprisingly accurate 5ft 2ins with golden brown skin. This is notably shorter than the Zomdickians, who were significantly taller than Earthlings. Shebic being Lilliput to Zomdic's Brobdingnag.[71] As for Shebic itself, it is almost defined by what it doesn't have with FSR reporting James as saying it had no industry and no birds.

Similarly to the Zomdickians, the Shebicians (my phrasing) do not return James to the place they picked him up from. Instead they drop him at Moore. Moore is 13 miles from Helsby Hill but in fairness it is closer to his home in Runcorn than Helsby, being around seven and a half miles from there.[72]

FSR does not mention the previous and much more in depth interview of 1958. The 1960 report merits much less space and consists of just two paragraphs in a section of

---

70 FSR, volume 6, number 2, 1960.
71 Jonathan Swift, *Gulliver's Travels*, 1726
72 www.theaa.com/route-planner

the journal called 'World round-up of news and comment about recent sightings'.

Intriguingly also in the 'World round-up section' is the story of a UFO sighting by a woman from New Ferry, Wirral. The sighting takes place on 24th November. If we had a specific date for James space launch from Helsby Hill, this arguably may give credence to his account in terms of some, admittedly loose, corroborative evidence. The person who saw the UFO, a Mrs M Sperring, of 30 Tilstock Avenue, says the craft, which was saucer shaped and topped with a flashing light atop a dome, after hovering in a stationery position, moved in the direction of Liverpool. Could this have been the craft James entered?

What conclusions can be drawn from James's tales? An examination of the basic premises and revelations do suggest what may have happened.

1. James is very much in the UFO contactee tradition and is not an abductee.
2. The message of living in a peaceful harmonious way with nature is 'New Age' in scope as of course is the reference to Aquarius in the name of his church.
3. James's story knits together both spiritualist and ufological tropes.
4. It is highly unlikely that his tale is literally true in the material sense.
5. His reporting of 'psychic vision' and Zomdic being 'beyond the spirit world' are more in keeping with a prophetic experience along the lines of Ezekiel.[73]

---

73 Book of Ezekiel, The Bible

In conclusion I simply think that James was attempting to promote his church and also update its positioning and appearance for the space age. His message was one of earthly peace and harmony, which would be particularly pertinent following the war ravaged first half of the century and the more hot than cold, Cold War.

The percentage guess is that James had a lucid dream or dreams of some sort and expanded and embellished them into a tale he thought may tap into the zeitgeist of science fiction and contacteeism, while also attracting more followers to his spiritualist group, something he held dear.

Dismissing him simply as a liar, I think misses the point and his significance. James believes that both his message and his spiritualism are vitally important. He may almost have convinced himself that he did travel 'in a way' to an alien world, based on visions from his 'trance state'. James is a product of, and contributor to, the outsider thought of his age, linking spiritualism to the exponentially growing phenomenon of UFO experiencers. He holds a mirror up to the state of the new age and outsider religious Garden of Eden at this point in time.

Four
The Swinging Sixties

> Turn on, Tune in, Drop out
> Timothy Leary

James changed tack slightly in the 1960s. From June 1961 he started referring to himself as 'The Most Illustrious Brother, the Reverend James Cooke, APh', pronouncing himself the head of the Aquarius group.[74]

July 1966 would see James hit the tabloids with both the *Sunday People* and the now happily defunct *News of The World* running scathing stories. The *Sunday People*'s headline about James and his cohorts being 'Crackpots in Dog Collars'. Being criticised by the British tabloid press isn't necessarily indicative of the target being in any way morally reprehensible of course. In fact the British tabloids criticising anyone often brings to mind a cannibal criticising somebody for eating battery farmed eggs.

In a way, I feel proud of James here. He is managing to make national news and to garner publicity for his group. The old Wildean ethos that 'there is only one thing in life worse than being talked about and that is not being talked about'[75] surely applies here.

The papers report that James and members of his group had taken to the Norfolk Broads, traipsing round

---

74 *Paranormal Merseyside*, S.D Tucker, 'Runcorn's First Space Traveller', Amberley, Stroud, 2013

75 *The Picture of Dorian Gray,* Oscar Wilde, first released, *Lippincott's Monthly Magazine*, July 1890

the area selling silver discs which they said had mystical powers, handing out religious pamphlets and also hitting the local ale houses bucket rattling for donations.

This is a peculiar recruitment drive, perhaps an extra/ultra-terrestial being or Chu-cha-ka has advised James that the Norfolk Broads would be a fruitful orchard for ripe converts. In any event it doesn't seem to have been enough to keep the Aquarian Crusades on the march and the group closed down in 1969, poetically of course the year humans landed on the moon.

In any event I returned to the source and ordered an original copy of the *Sunday People*, July 17, 1966.

Now, here I should say that I am not a particularly credulous person, despite my long standing passion for UFOs, the paranormal and Forteana in general. So I just mention this in passing. Largely as the result of auto-suggestion, I had noticed a number of odd incidences while writing up James's tale. If anyone ever reads this, they may recall that the title of Chapter 2 is *A Night to Remember*. I didn't give much thought to the chapter's title, it just seemed a natural fit.

The only way I could find to obtain an original *Sunday People* from that era was to order it through a gift service, costing over £60. On the morning of the day the paper arrived, my wife and myself were woken up at around 4.30am by our telephone landline ringing. This caused some temporary alarm as it is unprecedented for us to receive a call on the landline at this time in the morning, and having not reached the phone in time to answer, we had hastily reached for our mobiles to check for messages, fearing an accident had occurred or some other unwanted incident to a family member. But there was nothing. Checking the number we had been called on from the landline drew a blank. Number unknown.

Later that day, the *Sunday People* edition arrived. It came in a pleasant gift box and on that box was written 'A Day to Remember'. Also enclosed was a certificate of authentication. These of course were proffered by the company providing the archive newspapers as an added touch for newspapers being given as a gift. I would imagine that most people would put on the certificate 'presented to my loving aunt, on the occasion of the 50-year anniversary of your soufflé prize winning' and the like. As there was no extra cost for the certificate, I had requested, 'presented to Daniel Clay, on the occasion of Zomdic Contact, Zomdic contacted 60 years on'.

The whole phone call, night to remember – day to remember incident was one of a number of spooky coincidences which I will confirm did give me pause to ponder and raise a metaphorical eyebrow. My eyebrow would raise to Sir Roger Moore levels of elevation later that day.

Anyway, having opened up the paper and anticipating a short entry somewhere, I was surprised to see more or less half of page 4, of a Sunday Broadsheet paper, being devoted to James. This is almost nine years on from his Zomdic trip.

The first thing that leaps out is a black and white photograph of a grinning, radiant James Cooke. If anything he looks younger than his mugshot in the RWN of 1957 and round his neck hangs an elaborate bejewelled Star of David medallion. He is sporting a pure white dog collar and a charismatic mien. His hair is free, curly and receding. He looks like a perfect Dr Who composite. His wavy hair contrasts with the sensible severe side parting he sported in 1957. The hair was greyer yes but all the brighter for it.

Scholars of newspaper photography methods may just argue that the *Sunday People* picture is differently exposed or the like but I'm not sure. There is a more overt personality coming through in the 1966 snap.

In fact the two pictures work as a nice compare and contrast visual metaphor for the difference between the 1950s and 1960s. In the 1950s James has a sensible parting, dark hair and although he is smiling, he looks awkward and a bit like he is waiting for a whack across the wrists with a ruler. By 1966, he is working a decidedly bling medallion, his hair is freed from its shackles, his smile is warm and his face glowing.

The caption beneath the photograph states ''The Most Reverend' James Cooke – 'I've been called a phoney before', he said'.

There is also a close up picture of a Mrs Kathleen Hocknell, the 47-year-old wife of one of James's crew. A Mr & Mrs Hocknell were of course part of the group who greeted James on his return to Runcorn from Zomdic back in 1957.

The headline for the article is the somewhat leading 'Crackpots in Dog Collars…cruising down the river – to catch the mugs'. Not much chance of a fair or balanced hearing for The Aquarian Church then, it would appear.

Accompanying the story about James on page 4 are the TV listings for the day. If you were waking up on Sunday

Morning and fancied a bit of viewing, you would have the option of watching a morning service from St Peter's Cathedral, Geneva or a family worship service from the Congregational Church, Birkenhead. The Christian hegemony was in full effect. Journalist Michael Dale clearly had little time for James and his church, which is a shame given James has given up his time to him to be interviewed but I guess that is part of the still ongoing tabloid dance.

James, along with four other dog collared gents and the similarly attired Mrs Hocknell had been boating on the Norfolk Broads over the summer on a 40ft cruiser called Sea Earl.

Stopping regularly along the Broads, the crew would collect money from locals or tourists, telling them that the collection was for a 'church building fund'. The clear insinuation from Dale was that they were obtaining money under false pretences and that the people donating to them believed Cooke and his merry band were the type of people who would eagerly tune in to a family worship service from the Wirral, rather than tuning into the latest transmissions from a planet called Zomdic, brought to them by a supernatural incorporeal presenter called Chu-cha-ka.

Continuing his damnation of them, Dale states authoritatively that no church organisation he has spoken to has heard of The Aquarian Church.

James refers to himself immodestly as 'Most Eminent Divine', with the Sunday People preferring the somewhat less grandiose title of 'former furniture salesman'. His official Aquarian Church title is given as 'the Most

Illustrious Brother, the Most Reverand James Cooke, A Ph'. 'A.Ph' isn't a recognised qualification, with James indicating that he is a 'Doctor of Aquarian Philosophy', while conceding that only fellow members of The Aquarian Church recognise him as such.

The article places the HQ of the Aquarian Church at Bridge Street, Runcorn. Bridge Street is one of the main thoroughfares of the town. Again, the bridge totem is attaching itself to James. The HQ consists of a disused shop which logic would indicate may well have been his previous furniture shop.

On offer from the Aquarian Brotherhood are disc brooches which they sell for £5 a shot. That is some price in 1966. Bear in mind that it equates to around £65 in modern terms.[76] The average weekly wage was around £24 per week,[77] so James was asking people to part with a fifth of their weekly income for one of his mystically empowered brooches.

Booklets were available for 2s, around £2 in modern money.[78] The booklets invited the purchaser to co-operate with the Aquarian Healing Circle and its charitable work.

Also available were mystical cards which the user could fling to the floor in order to receive a special message. A pack of these cards cost two guineas, approximating to about fifty quid today. Oh for an original set of those cards! Although it did give me an idea for a bit of first hand research into contacting Zomdic. When I punched 'magickal word cards' (additional k intended) into a search

---

76 www.moneysorter.co.uk 13.5.17
77 www.sixties.net/Events/Events66
78 www.concertina.com

engine, the first page which showed up was for a retail organisation called Magic Words.[79] I hasten to add they produce important high quality educational word cards for children and are in no way involved in cartomancy of any kind. On their website homepage, the cards held up by a beaming attentive parent to two similarly smiling kids, spelled out the sentence 'I look up and see you'. Maybe Zomdic is subtlety calling after all, with this cartomantic message to watch the skies.

Cooke and his group were also able to provide messages for people from a higher being, costing 20 guineas. This is over £400 in today's money so presumably only hardcore believers would be willing to part with such a sum. Or unbelievably gullible people, depending on one's point of view.

It is suspicious that such messages were charged for. Medallions, booklets and cards presumably cost something in production value and costs need to be covered to allow the good work of the Aquarian Church to continue. I would assume channelled messages were free, in the material sense at least. It is questionable what the money free Zomdickians would have viewed of this profit making. One would think The Aquarian Church and their Zomdickian guides, would have been keen to spread the word without putting financial barriers in the way.

James also makes clear that the four men sleep in the forward berths of the Sea Earl, while Mrs Hocknell had the back four berths all to herself. I would imagine this is to avoid any notion of impropriety or sexual deviancy. Given her husband is there though, it begs a question of

---

79 www.magicwords.com

why this point is presented. Almost certainly this was the *Sunday People* journalist Dale, hinting at something more salacious than simply what he clearly felt were dodgy crackpots.

James gives a mixed report on the success of the enterprise saying that 'some days the collections were good, sometimes not so good'.

One underwhelmed person was Grace Peacock of Wroxham, Norfolk. She was in a hairdressers when James entered and told her he was part of an organisation that was working to unite all religions. Possibly he also wanted a wave put in his now pleasingly undulating mane. Mrs Peacock explained that when she asked James questions about religions, he didn't have the answers. Despite this she purchased a pamphlet and James was able to collect around 10 shillings (about £10 in today's parlance) from people at the hairdressers, for his brooches and pamphlets. This does indicate a certain entrepreneurial skill and ties into James' other occupations as Furniture and Grocery salesman. This builds on the picture of a charismatic, confident individual who was used to pitching his wares, relying on his salesmanship to achieve success.

Gilbert Tallowin, landlord of The New Inn, a local hostelry, noted that three of the men had visited the establishment for lunch 'laughing and drinking pints of beer and eating pies'. Look, we're from Runcorn, this is what we do, along with pondering the possibility of ET life and the otherworld. If you're looking for some sort of scandal involving beer and pies you're way off.

One of the barmen, Jimmy Sizer read one of the booklets proffered by James and his acolytes, delivering the damning verdict: "This is a lot of rubbish, you're a bunch of phoneys."

James is unfazed by such criticism. He tells Michael Dale: "I've been called a phoney before. That was when I was transported to another planet in a flying saucer." So we know that almost nine years on from his supposed trip to Zomdic, James was sticking to his guns about the tale.

He defends the Aquarian Church's practice of sporting dog collars saying: "Anyone can put on a dog collar and get away with it but I insist my people wear their discs." Even so, this does smack of duplicity as the dog collars will have equated to respectable Christianity to the people James was collecting money from.

There is a chance that the decision to take to the Norfolk Broads was in part due to James and The Aquarian Church needing to leave their usual North-West England locality. They may have acquired a reputation back in Runcorn and its surrounds, finding it difficult to raise funds.

The article though ends any doubt about James's position in the Aquarian Church. He is its leader. The *Sunday People* speaks to him. He refers to his congregational comrades as 'my people' and James has the authority to insist they wear the magickal discs.

Dale remarks that James and his 'brothers' may well hold their strange beliefs sincerely and that he may even be convinced he travelled in a flying saucer. The fact that a tabloid journalist who clearly holds great antipathy towards James, to the point of ridicule, is willing to state that he thinks James is convinced of his beliefs is very interesting. This is someone who has met and interviewed James, who is ill disposed towards him and his antics but who assesses that James is sincere in as much as he believes what he is saying.

Dale pithily says he himself has a sincere belief which is that James' group is a 'crackpot sect and anyone who gives it money in future must be a mug'. Thus the article ends, and as far as I can tell, any interest in James by the media.

One other interesting fact which comes out of the article is that the Aquarian Brothers wore purple cassocks. This along with him being largely derided for his views by the media brings to mind David Icke, although of course Icke favoured turquoise to purple, often sporting a suitably hued shell suit. Icke viewed turquoise as a conduit for positive energy.[80]

James presents as something of an underachiever. Icke went on to become one of the most prominent outsider thought advocates of his generation, with a prodigious output of literature and successful world tours. No such luck for James. Clearly something just wasn't quite falling into place for him, he couldn't quite get his coals to catch fire.

Maybe this derogatory article put James into a crisis of confidence, maybe the media thought there was nothing more to add and lost interest. Based on his earlier comments to the RWN in 1957 about expecting ridicule, I would have thought it would take more than a couple of scathing press articles to make him throw in the towel. Perhaps it was a bit much for some of his congregation, maybe the funds just dried up, probably a combination of the two. Either way, we know from his death certificate

---

80 *In the Light of Experience,* David Icke, 1993, Time Warner

that at some point over the next 30 years he turned to greengrocery.

This then is where is appears to end for James as a doyen of alternative religion in Britain. There is no further record of his activities, as far as I have been able to find, in the mainstream media or ufological cannon.

Tale of his exploits would continue to be regurgitated in ufology over the coming decades and through to the present day. The accounts would vary in accuracy but his original Zomdic tale from 1957 would see him cement his place in the lore of British ufology as its first 'abductee'. Not entirely accurate of course but arguably a fitting legacy.

FIVE
JAMES COOKE IN THE UFOLOGICAL LITERATURE

> This was the appearance and structure
> of the wheels: They sparkled like topaz,
> and all four looked alike.
> Each appeared to be made like a
> wheel intersecting a wheel.
> Ezekiel 1:16[81]

Here I will trace the chain of custody through the ufological literature and look at how the story has developed.

UFOs Operation Trojan Horse

In 1971, John Keel's *UFOs Operation Trojan Horse*[82] references James's tale. Keel is a significant figure in ufology, attributed with coining the phrase 'men in black' (MIB) when writing for adventure magazine *Saga* in his article *UFO Agents of Terror*.[83] He was awarded his own plaque commemorating him as 'Ufologist of the Year' in 1967, 10 years after James travelled to Zomdic.

---

81 *The Bible*, New International Version
82 *UFOs Operation Trojan Horse*, John Keel, 1971, Souvenir Press, London
83 https://en.wikipedia.org/wiki/John_Keel

The honour bestowed at the Convention of Scientific Ufologists[84].

He also authored the work *The Mothman Prophecies*[85], an investigation into a large winged harbinger of doom creature spooking the inhabitants of Point Pleasant, West Virginia and later turned into a successful film starring Richard Gere.[86]

In Trojan Horse, Keel incorrectly spells James's surname Cook, missing the 'e'. He does though correctly list James under 'Contactees' in his excellent index.

James features in a chapter titled *You Are Endangering the Balance of the Universe!* [87]

Keel describes James as a 'quiet gentleman'. However he does not present James's tale in the context of him already being steeped in spiritualism. He reports that James had seen an object in the sky which was oscillating between blue, white and dark red in colour. He provides a brief summation of James' story about his trip to Zomdic, saying that after the experience he 'quietly returned to his garden in the English countryside' and that like most known contactees he didn't write any books or go on any lecture tours.

Keel here is over-spicing the cake or under-flavouring it, either way he is doing something to the cake. James was not an unassuming genteel English man, fitting the overworked U.S. stereotype of a buttoned up, stiff upper

---

84 *UFOs Operation Trojan Horse*, ibid
85 *Visitors From Space the Astonishing True Story of the Mothman Prophecies*, John Keel, 1975, Panther Books,
86 *The Mothman Prophecies*, Director Mark Pellington, Lakeshore Entertainment 2002
87 Ibid, pages 199-214

lipped, walking bowler hat. He was a member of The Aquarian Crusades spiritualist group and more than happy to recount his tales to members of the press.

Keel also says that James showed Flying Saucer reporter Miss Roberts the burn on his hand from touching the Zomdickain craft's rail. This isn't reported by FSR[88], Miss Roberts notes that a Mr E. Thomas who was there when James returned to Runcorn from his trip, saw the burn.

Keel notes that an Argentine airman had reported receiving a similar message to James from ET one month earlier in August 1957. An unnamed member of the Argentinian Air Force was sent as part of a three man plane crash retrieval team to a location near Quilino in Cordoba, Argentina. He stayed behind at the base camp they had set up while the other two members of the team, went for supplies.

Hearing a hum he exited the tent to be greeted by the sight of a huge disc hovering overhead. He tried to draw his pistol but was unable to. A soft voice told him not to worry and mentioned that the aliens had a base for their craft in nearby Salta province. They had a message for him, not dissimilar to the one James came back with from Zomdic, namely 'we intend to help you, for the misuse of atomic energy threatens to destroy you'.

The story was picked up by a respected and popular Argentinian newspaper *Diaro de Cordoba*. Keel notes James had never heard the Argentinian story but I doubt he could have been certain.

Keel is well known for this theories about 'ultraterrestrials' and *Operation Trojan Horse* develops

---
[88] *FRS* vol 4, no 4 ibid

these ideas. He writes compellingly about the concept of the human mind being linked to a greater whole, similar in concept to the Jungian theory of a collective subconscious but expanding this to include para-physical beings who can manipulate the human psyche through falsification of memory, telepathic messages and psychic attacks.

This would appear to chime with James's tale and Keel utilises him as a small building block in his theory that such beings are ultraterrestials or elemental beings. Keel refers to the experiences that humans are subjected to by the ultraterrestials as 'confabulations'.[89] The ultraterrestial denizen is able to manipulate the human mind and implant psychic experiences therein. This is a sympathetic appraisal of James' reports and it is heartening that Keel doesn't just simply dismiss him as a Jackanory dream weaver. If James was sensitive to such ultraterrestials, they may have been communicating to him through his psychic vision, imparting information and images while making him believe he had an actual material experience. James seems to suspect himself that this may have been the case with his comments about his Zomdic experience taking place beyond the spiritual world in a world of thought.

Of course these days, there are myriad theories about infinite numbers of parallel dimensions and the possibilities of beings travelling between these dimensions. Perhaps James had genuine psychic encounters with such denizens.

Keel covers a vast range of stories and reports of alien visitation and communication, both in the abductee and contactee tradition. A true giant of ufology.

---

89 *UFOs Operation Trojan Horse*, ibid, pages 301-302

Notable Compilation Entries

As noted earlier, James receives 11 lines in *The UFO Encyclopedia*.[90]

He benefits from greater investigation in *The Mammoth Book of UFOs*.[91] Compiler Lynn Picknett has picked up the trail from John Keel's account in *UFOs Operation Trojan Horse*[92] and generally bases her account on Keel's. The section is headed *7 September 1957, Runcorn, Cheshire, England* and features in a chapter of the book called The Invaders.

Picknett proposes that James may have had his only ever episode of temporal lobe epilepsy (TLE). Interesting speculative theory though this is, we can discount it as a one-time only occurrence for James as of course he also went on another inter-galactic trip in November 1959 to Shebic.[93]

Picknett notes that TLE has been known to induce mystical and religious experiences in people. There are no reports I can find that James had this condition and my reading of the evidence we have is that his stories were far more pre-meditated in that they were intended to promote his spiritualist group. If James did suffer from TLE this would cast an interesting light on the context of his experience but there is no evidence for this, just guesswork that this may be behind the UFO and spiritual experiences which he had.

---

90 Ibid
91 Ibid
92 Ibid, pages 67-69
93 *FSR* vol 6, no 2, ibid

1990s

Little escapes phenomenal UFO researcher Jenny Randles's attention. James is noted in her *Mysteries of the Mersey Valley*, released in 1993 and written with Peter Hough, in a chapter titled *Through the looking glass, via Zomdic*.[94] One slight quibble with the misspelling of his name aside, the 'e' being omitted from Cooke, the title is a nice summation.

Forty-five hours is given as the length of time for James's trip.

Randles and Hough propose that some of the lights he saw may have been airplanes travelling to nearby Speke (now Liverpool John Lennon) airport.

This may account for any number of sightings in the Runcorn area. Motorists who have travelled in North-West England will be familiar with signs saying 'For Liverpool Airport follow Runcorn', with frequent flights ascending or descending over the town. Intriguingly Randles and Hough deny Cooke the title of being Britain's first alien traveller, bestowing this honour on George King. More on King can be found in the following chapter *Contactees*.

Having looked into King however, it appears to me that although he undoubtedly professed to be in contact with alien beings, he did not claim that he had travelled to their worlds, in a material sense at least, prior to James's trip to Zomdic in 1957. Like George Adamski, King claimed that his contacts initially came to visit him from their home base on Venus, as opposed to a world unknown to astrophysicists.

---

94 *Mysteries of the Mersey Valley*, Peter Hough & Jenny Randles, 1993, Sigma Leisure, Wilmslow

Millennial accounts

Damning James with the faint praise of being 'one of the least known British contactees', in *Flying Saucerers: A Social History of Ufology*[95] by David Clarke and Andy Roberts, James's tale is examined within the social context of the Cold War. They note how Cooke's position altered in a nuanced manner from claiming experiences similar to George Adamski to being more in alignment with George King who founded The Aetherius Society (see chapter 6 – *Contactees*).

They contrast the Zomdickian aliens and other galactic beings of the 1950s with the somewhat cruel 'grey' alien types which would come to prominence in the 1980s. This they interpret as an understandable psychological reaction to the grim realities of the Cold War, with the unending possibility that humankind was only one four-minute warning away from total annihilation.

They note that stories of contact with alien races provide escapism. I would also add there would have been deep unconscious and conscious desires for higher intelligences to come down and help humankind extricate itself from the seemingly inexorable path to destruction on which it had set itself.

Insightfully, Clarke and Roberts also outline their theory that the harmonious and equable societies the aliens had was a way of people reinterpreting the threat of Communism in a kinder manner – presumably to take the sting out of the threat and maybe also as a form of

---

95 *Flying Saucerers*, David Clarke & Andy Roberts, 2007, Alternative Albion, Loughborough

psychological protectionism with the inference that if the reds finally did take over the world, maybe it wouldn't be as bad as feared.

They also present more detail about the practices of James's Church of Aquarius, saying that attendees at the church would sit around a luminous plate in a dark room to receive their visions. Clarke and Roberts feel that James was a genuine believer and their conclusion that he was essentially a spiritualist trying to move with the times and replace spirits with aliens, chimes with my own.

They also say that James's church group met in a converted shop.

James's Reggie Perrin-style rise and fall is also outlined as they follow him to his ridicule at the hands of the *News of the World* and *Sunday People* in the mid-1960s. They describe how after this, James faded from public view before dying in obscurity.

Indeed thinking of James and his group of Aquarian utopians on a boating holiday in the Norfolk Broads, certainly brings to mind the classic British sit-com *The Fall and Rise of Reginald Perrin*.[96] Perrin establishes a house based utopian cult in a London suburb. Perrin's aim is less grandiose than James, he just wants 'better, happier, people'.[97] Much in the same way one can imagine James's dreams and group being ransacked by the merciless British tabloids, the house which doubles as the headquarters of Perrin's group is sacked by people who have personal gripes with his 'Perrin's Peace Keeping Force'.

In fact having spent a lot of time absorbing James, his

---

96 *The Fall and Rise of Reginald Perrin*, BBC television, 1976-1979
97 Ibid, series 3, 1978-1979

tales and the images presented of him, it occurs to me that Leonard Rossiter who played Reginald Perrin would have been perfect for playing James. Alas it is never to be.

SD Tucker provides a nice tight and informative chapter on James in his *Paranormal Merseyside* released in 2013.[98] It is heartening that the tale is still notable, certainly in terms of local mysteries, cementing his place in the folklore of North West England.

Other than the examples mentioned above, he has received little attention. There is no blue plaque in Westfield Road and as previously mentioned he doesn't have a Wikipedia entry. Internet search engines will see him present in many UFO and paranormal enclaves but these generally briefly rehash the usual inaccurate version of the tale that he was abducted and set up a UFO cult church before vanishing.

The year 2017, the 60th anniversary of James's trip to Zomdic did see a flurry of interest. A pop-up museum in the town celebrated James's tale as well as UFOs in Runcorn generally.[99] I was lucky enough to visit this excellent installation which had a good deal of information about James and other UFO sightings in the Runcorn area.

---

98 *Paranormal Merseyside*, Ibid
99 http://www.liverpoolecho.co.uk/whats-on/whats-on-news/ufo-museum-opens-runcorn-ahead-12879220

SIX
Contactees

> It seems to me now incredibly wonderful that, with that swift fate hanging over us, men could go about their petty concerns as they did.
> *The War of the Worlds* – H G Wells[100]

The history of humankind communicating with beings of supposedly higher intelligence was of course not only decades old but centuries old by the time James chewed the fat about humankind's appetite for destruction in the 1950s.

Arguably the first reported contact with higher intelligence occurred when naked humans Adam and Eve, had a strange interaction with a talking serpent in the Garden of Eden.[101] Unlike later interactions, this particular being did not tell the humans to be nice to each other. Seemingly they had a more divisive message.

One notable result of this interaction with Adam and Eve, the original 'Betty and Barney Hill'[102], is that they decided to eschew their nudity and throw some clothes on.

As an aside, it is notable that although this instruction to wear clothing is presumably to many of a religious bent,

---

100 Wells, HG, *The War of the Worlds,* 1898, William Heinemann, London
101 *The Bible,* Genesis, author and date disputed
102 The Hills were famously abducted in 1961 by Zeta Reticuli aliens, e.g their entry in *The UFO Encyclopedia* ibid

Satanic in origin, full on nudity is largely absent from the mainstream religions.

As a further and tenuously spooky aside, I picked up an old copy of a *Good News Bible*.[103] I have had since a child to see if I could find some direct quotes from said talking serpent but the page they would be on in this particular edition, p5-6, had been removed or was never there. The page was surgically removed, no sign of ripping or anything like that. Strange indeed. Read into that what you will. Perhaps Cha-chu-ka had spirited it away, not wanting me to liken the Zomdickians to the Adversary.

In any event, I think most people are familiar with the tale which involved the snake telling Eve to live a little and eat an apple which the human creator God had specifically told them not to eat. This doesn't go down well. God basically goes nuts, cursing the snake, introducing childbirth pain and taking a line of general misogyny, saying 'I will make your pains in childbearing very severe; with painful labour you will give birth to children, your desire will be for your husband and he will rule over you'. All very disproportionate, uncompassionate and unnecessary you would think. Presumably if you are a theologian of intellect you will view this as allegorical rather than in any way literal and I would bow to your greater knowledge. Probably.

I include it here though to show how such communications with higher intelligence, however seemingly outlandish at face value, are not always just dismissed out of hand as nonsensical ramblings.

---
103 *Good News Bible*, British & Foreign Bible Society, London, 1976

Religious works are of course chock full of tales of communications with higher intelligence although these are interpreted as deific in nature rather than supposedly material beings from outer space. The likes of Erich von Daniken[104] and Graham Hancock have of course provided fascinating alternative interpretations of religious texts.[105]

George Adamski

Polish immigrant and onetime prohibition booze bootlegger, George Adamski, is generally regarded as the founding father of the UFO contactee tradition.

The contactee tradition had been in full swing in the USA since the early 1950s and at the time of James's journeys to Zomdic and Shebic respectively was a hot ticket for booksellers.

My second hand copy of Desmond Leslie and George Adamski's *Flying Saucers Have Landed* is a seventh edition released in March 1954. The first edition had only been released in September 1953.[106] It was selling like hot cakes, presumably on hot saucers.

James's significance is in him being, as far as can be told from the reports and ufological literature, the first person attempting to replicate the Adamski driven contactee model in Europe. James claims not just to have been in contact with the aliens psychically but like Adamski to have travelled to their world.

---

104 *Chariots of the Gods,* ibid
105 *Fingerprints of the Gods*, Graham Hancock, 1995 Reed, London
106 *Flying Saucers Have Landed,* D Leslie & G Adamski, 1953, T Werner Laurie, London

Adamski also backed up his claims with photographs and film footage of his experiences. The photographs would show pictures of the alien craft and other oddities such as alien writing.

He is defiant with regard to scepticism of the flying saucer phenomenon, citing the overwhelming amount of sightings and photographs as indisputable evidence. His photographs have often been dismissed as simply close-ups of lamp shades and the like. However, his initial shouts about alien contact still echo down through the ufological canyon to this day.

Setting the contactee stall out, he also concludes that the beings from the other worlds are benevolent towards humankind, wanting to protect us from ourselves and preserve the cosmic balance.[107]

Adamski's first experience with alien beings came as a result of an excursion into the Mojave Desert to look for UFOs. He saw a number of crafts and unusually in the world of paranormal experiencers, was able to take a number of photographs.

Direct contact came in the form of Orthon, a being from Venus of whom Adamski said, 'the beauty of his form surpassed anything I had ever seen'. Orthon came from Venus and had decided to make the trip to planet Earth to warn humankind about the twin dangers of nuclear weaponry and pollution.

Like other contactees, Adamski is anxious not to tread on the toes of the established main Earth religions, suggesting 'Orthodox Christians need have no trouble with their beliefs in accepting the idea of extra-terrestrial

---

107 *Flying Saucers Have Landed*, pg 221

humanities'.[108] Instead he explains that the equivalent of the biblical 'fall of man', the transition of humans from the Garden of Eden to the world of sin, did not occur on Venus. This gave them an advanced utopian society and a desire to assist their little brother Earthlings in reaching an equivalent idyll.

Adamski has provoked a wide-ranging reaction from sceptics, who point out that in addition to his alien spacecrafts looking suspiciously like lampshades and the like, that it isn't possible for human like creatures to live on Venus. However, he certainly made waves and reflected the desire of people to read this type of literature, in a very uncertain age.

In 1965 he would die of a heart attack at the age of 74, shortly after delivering a lecture on his theories in Maryland, USA.[109]

Daniel Fry/Rolf Telano

Closely following Leslie and Adamski's seminal release, Daniel Fry's *The White Sands Incident: An Extraterrestial Statement* was released in 1954.[110]

Fry was employed at the White Sands Proving Ground, New Mexico. White Sands is still a missile testing range for the US military today. While working, Fry saw a large flying saucer land nearby. Venturing over to investigate,

---

108 Ibid page 165

109 www.signonsandiego.com:80/news/northcounty/20030813-9999_7m13ufo.html

110 *The White Sands Incident,* Daniel Fry, 1954, New Age (my copy Horus House Press 1992, Wisconsin)

he was about to place his hand on the craft when a voice warned him 'better not touch the hull pal, it's still hot!'

Two things here. Firstly the idea of a hot craft and use of the terminology 'pal' sounds all too human.

Secondly it resonates with James' experience of entering and exiting the saucer on his trip to Zomdic. James of course claimed to have burned his hand when exiting the craft and also to have been given advice on how to safely embark and disembark, from a disembodied voice.

This can be interpreted in a number of different ways. It could give credence to James's story. After all this is another individual, on a different continent, who has reported that the saucers are hot and the occupants shout out instruction on how to proceed safely around the craft.

Cynically, it could be concluded that James was familiar with the contactee literature emanating from the United States and being aware of the groundswell of popularity for this type of thing, was drawing on the accounts to create tales for his own ends.

The similarity of the accounts continues. Fry is contacted by an alien called A-lan, who soon drops the pretentious hyphen in his name in favour of the far more down-to-earth Alan. Alan takes Fry off in a saucer to his home planet. There he instructs Fry to take back a message for humankind warning them of the dangers of nuclear war.

Telano writes profoundly and eloquently on the human condition of perma-war and the rationale for people like Fry relaying the messages they do, under tutelage of Alan. For example 'the tragedy and futility of warfare lie in the fact that it cannot determine the relative merits of the conflicting ideologies, it can only demonstrate the relative fighting abilities of the participants!'[111]

Also 'mankind today finds a tiny beach beside a vast sea of ignorance, superstition, greed and inhumanity. The beach exists because, down through the ages, countless billions of brave souls crawled out of the sea for a moment at least, and each brought with him a few grains of sand which he left behind. We can do no less than to add our few grains of sand, that we may leave the beach just a little larger than we found it – until at long last, some day in the dim future, the beach will be large enough to contain all of mankind, and none will be forced to remain unwilling in the sea.'[112] Some may find the metaphor somewhat overworked but I think it reveals a heartfelt and sincere desire, shared with James and the wider contactee movement of the 1950s, to guide humankind away from the path of self-destruction it was set on, towards a brighter more harmonious future for all.

Indeed, it is tempting to dismiss the contactees as at best harmless fantasists and at worst fraudulent charlatans. When you return to their actual writing, however, if nothing else the sincerity of their vision and desire for a better world comes through strongly. Admittedly this may be from their own deep held desires for a more just and equable world, rather than a higher intelligence but their motivation is sincere. What grains of sand will any of us leave behind for those who want a better place to live on and societies to live in?

---

111 Ibid, Horus House edition page 30

112 *The White Sands Incident*, Horus edition page 92

George King

Certainly the most important British contactee of the 1950s was Dr George King. King beat James to the punch as Britain's first alien contactee by three years. He was contacted by an alien being called 'Aetherius' in 1954[113].

King founded the Aetherius Society which has stood the test of time and still has a global presence today.

On a Saturday morning in May 1954, Dr King heard a voice which said 'prepare yourself! You are to become the voice of Interplanetary Parliament'.

It is worth mentioning that like James, Dr King did not go from being a down-to-earth taxi driver[114] to a pioneer of alien contacteeism in a flash of revelation. Dr King was a Quaker in his youth and a conscientious objector during the Second World War, although assisting the British Fire Service during the blitz.

It was during this time that he developed an interest in the more esoteric forms of yoga, devoting many hours to the likes of mantra and kundalini yoga. Through this practise, by the mid-1950s, he had developed finely attuned psychic abilities.

A few days later an international yoga master visited Dr King. The yoga master boasted the ability of being able to pass through locked doors without opening them and he continued with Dr King's yogic training and development. Dr King founded the Aetherian Society in 1955.

King began to produce 'transmissions' from higher

---

113 www.aetherius.org/dr-george-king/
114 *Mysteries of the Mersey Valley*, P Hough & J Randles, 1993, Sigma Leisure, Wilmslow

beings, issuing messages for humankind. Many of these beings but not all, came from other planets. The main source of the transmissions was a being known as Master Aetherius who resided on Venus.

Of course the likelihood of life as we understand it being present on Venus is unlikely and the Aetherius Society recognise this in their official output.[115] However, they maintain that such beings can be contacted by projecting from the physical body and tuning into a higher frequency. Dr King would channel the transmissions either telepathically or when in a trance state, which certainly chimes with James's reflections on his contact with the beings of Zomdic and his postulation that they came from 'beyond the spirit world'.

Dr King passed away in 1997 aged 78.

The Aetherius Society established a key branch of theirs in Warrington, a neighbouring town of Runcorn. They still detail contacts for both Warrington and Liverpool on their website, although sadly neither responded to my email enquiries about James.

It is hard to assess how much of Dr King and The Aetherius Society's teachings influenced James. He would certainly have been aware of their presence and philosophy.

In some ways it is tempting to see James as an underachiever, attempting to replicate more successful contactee groups such as The Aetherius Society and ultimately coming up short. It is intriguing though that he did not simply merge with or join the group and I think this is due to his desire to continue along the path

---

115 www.aetherius.org

of Spiritualism, incorporating elements of the brand new alien based contacteeism. He did not wish to replace it completely.

Orfeo Angelucci and Carl Jung

Orfeo Angelucci was an American contactee, also prominent in the 1950s. In his book *The Secret of the Saucers*[116] he outlines that beginning in 1952, when driving home from his work at an aircraft factory in California, he encountered 'flying saucers' piloted by aliens with a general human appearance.

The book was edited by Ray Palmer, the driving force behind *Fate Magazine*. *Fate Magazine* had been pivotal in the history of ufology, carrying Kenneth Arnold's eponymous flying saucer tale in 1948.[117]

His first contact occurred in May 1952. Two globe shaped craft disengaged from the flying saucer, with a voice advising him not to be afraid, similar to the reassurance given to Cooke when he tentatively approached the craft to take him to Zomdic. He was also provided with a crystal cup containing a restorative and fortifying beverage. The drink and its vessel materialising out of thin air. Again this resonates with Cooke's account of the extraterrestrials being able to produce material items out of thin air and also the viscous drink he received from the Zomdickians.

---

116 *The Secret of the Saucers*, Orfeo Angelucci, ed. Ray Palmer, Amherst Press, Wisconsin
117 *Fate Magazine*, February 1948

A screen appeared on which there was an image of two good-looking beings who Angelucci could sense were reading his thoughts. He had a further mental experience of a similar kind in July 1952, followed by actual contact with the alien beings on 2nd August 1952.

The message the aliens passed to him was slightly more apocalyptic than the ones channelled to the likes of Cooke and King. Angelucci was informed that a third world war was imminent. From the ruins of this Armageddon though, a new age would begin, rising phoenix like from the ashes of the ravaged Earth.

During his experiences with the alien beings, Angelucci came to realise that he himself had lived on an alien world in a past life. His name there was Neptune.

Angelucci attracted the attention of luminary of psychological thought Carl Jung, who referenced his experiences in *Flying Saucers: A Modern Myth of Things seen in the Sky*.[118]

Jung viewed flying saucer sightings as psychological representations of mandalas in the human subconscious, stating 'they are symbols, representing in visual form, some thought that was not thought consciously'.[119] He said of Angelucci that he 'has described in the greatest detail the mystic experience associated with a UFO vision' and that his story 'could be regarded as a unique document that sheds a great deal of light on the genesis and assimilation of UFO mythology'.[120]

---

118 *Flying Saucers: A modern myth of things seen in the sky*, Carl Jung, Princeton, 1978
119 Ibid page 19
120 Ibid page 117

While I don't agree that Angelucci's accounts are particularly unique, they are fascinating and can easily be interpreted as an expression of humankind's desire for a better world. One thing that as far as we can tell, is unique, is humankind. Angelucci and his fellow 1950s contactees wanted a better world than the nuclear fixated, divided, genocidal one that had dominated the first half of the 20th century. It is worth reflecting that while they were given short shrift by most, the world their fellow humans had created was a veritable Hell on Earth for many. Their vision was for an end to human suffering and a more humane place for all to exist.

Jung wrote masterfully when reflecting on the subject in his biography *Memories, Dreams, Reflections*.[121] His premise is that from a psychological point of view, the increasing cleft between humankind and their awareness of God takes the form of a circular symbol of unity in the unconscious. This circle is a mandala in the collective human subconscious, representing a healing of the self.

Jung outlines that he had come across this mandala representing a healing of the self in 1918 during the course of his investigations into the collective unconscious. This circular image 'represents the wholeness of the psychic ground, or to put it in mythic terms, the divinity incarnate in man'.[122]

He views the circular shaped UFOs as a manifestation of this mandala. This is particularly pertinent to contactees

---

121 *Memories, Dreams, Reflections*, Carl Jung, 1963, Collins and Routledge & Kegan Paul
122 Ibid. Page 367 in author copy published 1987, Fontana, London

who indeed seemed intent on healing the divisions present within humanity and putting them back in touch with a higher intelligence. Jung is sympathetic to the contactees, believing broadly speaking that what they are witnessing are manifestations of this unconscious mandala. He comments 'the worldwide stories of the UFOs are evidence of that; they are the symptom of a universally present psychic disposition'.

It also occurs to me that the halos present in many images of antiquity and right through to the present day, taken by ancient astronaut theorists as images of well, ancient astronauts, could also be interpreted as the manifestation of the unconscious desire for humanity to heal its internal rifts. Or of course, they could be images of the space-helmeted beings who had provided them with the blueprints and methods by which to construct the Giza pyramid complex and the like.

There is evidence for Jung's theory in Angelucci's own reflections and assertions based on his extra-terrestrial experiences. In *The Secret of the Saucers*, Angelucci writes 'if only every man and woman upon Earth could but grasp the great essential basic truth that *we are all one and an integral part of God* (his italics), then indeed all of mankind's hard trials and bitter tribulations would be over'.[123] This links directly to Jung's assertion that visions of saucers are psychological manifestations of the unconscious desire to heal the self and moreover the rift between the self and the divine.

Angelucci would die in Los Angeles on 24th July

---

123 *The Secret of the Saucers*, Ibid, Chapter 8 'My Awakening on Another Planet' page 112-13

1993, just six days before James Cooke. Like James his visionary comet had long faded from view by the time of his demise.

George Van Tassel

George Van Tassel was another American who met travelling space beings from Venus. Rather than merely passing on general messages regarding nuclear weaponry (bad) and harmonious peaceful living (good), the Venusians in this instance were keen to impart more practical information.

Bringing to mind somewhat the 'Orgasmatron' from Woody Allen's *Sleeper*,[124] in 1953 Van Tassel was invited on board a Venusian flying saucer for tuition in the construction of an 'Integratron'. The Integratron had loftier aims than the somewhat soulless instant sexual gratification offered by the Orgasmatron however.

Van Tassel described it thus, 'a time machine for basic research on rejuvenation, anti-gravity and time travel'.[125] He also commented: "The Integratron is a machine, a high voltage electro-static generator that would supply a broad range of frequencies to recharge the cell structure."[126]

In any event, here is was, an actual structure based supposedly on alien technology, a nuts and bolts structure, the first to be carried out under the instruction of a

---

124 *Sleeper*, Dir Woody Allen, written by Woody Allen and Marshall Brickman, United Artists, 1973
125 www.labyrinthina.com/amazing-integratron-at-giant-rock.html
126 https://integratron.com/history-of-the-integratron/

higher intelligence, since say The Pyramids, the Ark of the Covenant and the like, if you subscribe to the ancient alien or 'was God an astronaut?' theory.[127] It looks rather like a dessert, a muffin-shaped structure of two floors with the first floor appearing twice as tall as the ground one. Windows are positioned on both floors, also lending it an Adamski UFO like appearance.

As for the proof in this particular pudding? Well there is no record of any time travel, anti-gravity or Lazarus-like revenants having emerged from it but who's to say. The structure was built in Landers, California, and is still in use to this day.

Van Tassel was well equipped to construct such a structure. An aeronautical engineer by profession, he had worked for both the Douglas Aircraft company based in Southern California and as a test pilot for legendary eccentric and reclusive billionaire Howard Hughes at Hughes Aviation.[128] He also claimed to have drawn on the ideas of other visionary engineers such as Serbian-American Nikola Tesla.[129]

The project to construct the Integratron began in 1953 on a small scale, with the main work beginning in 1957, the year that James Cooke travelled to Zomdic. The structure was broadly completed by 1959 although as late as 1969, Van Tassel was still looking for financing with an official release explaining 'sub-assemblies are finished

---

127 *Chariots of the Gods: Was God an Astronaut?* Erich Von Daniken ibid

128 As opposed to personal fave Howard Hughes who presents *The Unexplained* podcast. Check it out now.

129 www.integratron.com

and we are now in the final assembly stage'.[130] Van Tassel also made clear through his regular releases from The College of Universal Wisdom that the intention was for the Integratron to be free for people wishing to use it, once completed.

In the final *Proceedings of the College of Universal Wisdom* release for 1969, Van Tassel likens the workings of the machine to the Kings Chamber in the Great Pyramid, asserting that this chamber was designed to revive dead VIPs in no more than three days if they had failed to come back to life (spontaneously presumably which seems unlikely). He also explains that the Kings Chamber had been deliberately built off-centre so as to access the correct energy for such resurrection. He is comfortable in confidently claiming that the whole process to resurrect an Egyptian VIP took 28 days. I take it as read that he received this information through his communications from his alien contacts although he doesn't specify.

He has a defiant message for the scientists of his day who he says 'in their two dimensional electro-magnetic science, cannot accept the fact that a handful of people today, understand this third plane of reference'. The third plane in question he describes as 'This Other Energy', which had also been used in the past to levitate people and other objects around, which of course would have helped with the construction of the Pyramids of Egypt and various other sites of wonder such as Stonehenge.

Van Tassel wasn't just the aliens' choice of chief engineer

---

130 *Proceedings of the College of Universal Wisdom*, Oct-Dec 1969, Yucca Valley California

for the mid-20th century, they also had a moral message they wanted him to deliver to humanity. Like his fellow 1950s contactees, he would bemoan the bad decisions that humanity had taken which had led to children starving, poverty and war. One key message from his extraterrestrial contacts was 'when they explode the hydrogen atom, they shall extinguish life on this planet, they are tinkering with a formula they do not comprehend'.[131]

His message was similar in essence to his peers in the contactee movement. However his unique feature was the fact that he was putting his – well, also other people's – money, where the aliens' mouths were and constructing something solid.

He would author a number of books based on his contactee experiences, two of which had been released by the time James Cooke reported on his trip to Zomdic, namely *I Rode in a Flying Sauce* (1952)[132] and *Into This World and Out Again*'[133] (1956). In March 1954 he staged the inaugural Interplanetary Spacecraft Convention in the Mojave Desert, California. Attendees included scientists and others with interest in the UFO phenomenon. Life Magazine reported on the event, gently chiding the attendees for their credulousness.[134] The contactee snowball was gathering weight however and attention from high circulation journals would only aid and abet this. By the time of the third Interplanetary

---

131 www.labyrinthina.com/amazing-integratron-at-giant-rock
132 George W Van Tassel, *I Rode in a Flying Saucer,* 1952, New Age Publishing Co, Los Angeles
133 George W Van Tassel, *Into this World and Out Again*, 1956, The College of Universal Wisdom, Yucca Valley
134 *Life Magazine,* 27 May 1957

Spacecraft Convention, almost 11,000 people and who knows what other beings, would attend.[135]

Some credence was given to Van Tassell's tales of interplanetary contact through his ability to predict UFO appearances. In June 1952 he wrote to *Life Magazine*, The *Los Angeles Herald Examiner* and the United States Air Force, informing them that extraterrestrial craft would soon fly over Washington DC. The letters were sent registered as proof. The letters would later be published in his book *When Stars Look Down*[136]. The following month, July 1952, Washington DC would experience a wave of UFO incidents. The UFOs in question were tracked on radar by both Washington National Airport and Andrews Air Force Base.[137] They were of particular interest as they had been tracked flying over The White House.

United States Air Force jets were scrambled to intercept the craft. At this point the craft would disappear, then reappear when the jets had returned to base. This convinced Harry Barnes, senior air traffic controller at Washington National Airport that the craft were monitoring and responding to, the actions taken by the Earthlings on the ground.[138]

When Stars Look Down is also notable for a truly peculiar theory regarding the Bermuda Triangle phenomenon. The Bermuda or 'Devil's' Triangle is

---

135 www.labyrinthina.com/amazing-integratron-at-giant-rock.html
136 *When Stars Look Down*, George Van Tassell, The Krukeberg Press, 1976, Los Angeles
137 *The UFO Encyclopaedia,* ibid, p 319
138 www.washingtoncitypaper.com/news/article/13023374/saucers-full-of-secrets

a triangular area, with its points at roughly Florida, Bermuda and Puerto Rico. Van Tassell is keen to defend Earth's alien visitors, asserting that they have nothing to do with the missing ships and planes which had vanished without trace.

His explanation is instead a very complicated geological theory relating to the anti-gravitational effects of quartz crystals on craft in the area, which he claims levitate ships and planes off and up into space.[139]

Van Tassell would die of a suspected heart attack on 9th February 1978.

Other notable 1950s contactees

Howard Menger was another contactee who claimed to have had alien experiences from his childhood onwards. Like Adamski he initially claimed that his ET friends hailed from Venus. His first meeting with an alien being came aged 10, in 1932.[140]

Menger claimed the alien had the appearance of a beautiful girl with long hair, wearing a see-through ski suit and emanated feelings of love. She advised Menger she was contacting others of her own kind.[141] This is an enigmatic comment, which I presume is intended to mean the alien wanted to contact other beings of a similar mindset rather than that Menger himself was an alien being.

---

139 *When Stars Look Down*, 'The Bermuda Triangle', p 194-198
140 'New York Day by Day' *Reading Eagle* (USA) May 17, 1957
141 *The UFO Encyclopaedia*, ibid, p 211

Menger's tales do have a slightly Leslie Phillips 'I say, ding dong'[142] feel to them. He had numerous encounters with attractive alien females wearing see through outfits. Menger claims to have offered them bras to wear, only for them to respond by telling him they didn't wear underwear.[143]

Later on in his life Menger would clarify his position on where the aliens came from, describing that rather than Venus being their homeworld, they were using it as a base of operations in the Solar System[144].

It is suggested that he recanted his tales of alien contact when appearing on TV in 1960, saying that he had been involved in a covert military operation aimed at gauging public reaction to tales of ET contact.[145]

The American military has unquestionably used the stories of flying saucer sightings percolating around society as a smokescreen for their own black ops programmes. For a full exposition of this, read the book and see the film of the superb *Mirage Men*.[146] An Air Force Office of Special Investigations (AFOSI) operative called Richard Doty had been integral in spreading misinformation aimed at discrediting and, disturbingly, mentally destroying witnesses to UFOs.

The distilled version of the theory is that by

---

142 See for example his character Jack Bell in 'Carry On Nurse', 1959 Dir: Gerald Thomas
143 *From Outer Space to You*, Howard Menger, Saucerian, 1959
144 UFO Secret: Alien Contacts Feature Film, UFOTV (available on You Tube)
145 http://strangeattractor.co.uk/news/howard-mengers-final-journey/
146 *Mirage Men,* Dir John Lundberg, 2013, Perception Management. Book: Mark Pilkington, 2010, Constable & Robinson

discrediting people claiming to have seen flying saucers, the public ignores the reports of sightings, believing them to be the ravings of cranks and the deluded. They also don't focus on what such witnesses are seeing, namely beyond top secret military tech. This muddies the waters on the subject so the fact cannot be separated from the fiction. The military operates behind this screen of misinformation. Exactly what they are hiding is of course the big question.

Menger had at one time in his life, been employed by the U.S. military, joining the 17th Tank Battalion after he left high school.[147] It is possible that he was used by the US military as a pawn to spread disinformation aimed at discrediting and confusing the public perceptions of purported alien contact. I doubt, however, he would have been so forthcoming with his revelations about this, so shortly after his engagement with it. That said, as *Mirage Men* reveals, this type of activity had occurred.

It casts another theory with regard to the contactees, in that some of them could have been military plants aimed at discrediting the wider UFO community and theories.

Menger died in 2009, aged 87 at his Florida home.

Aladino Felix was a Brazilian operating under the name **Dino Kraspedon** who, departing from the usual postulation of Venus as the homeworld of his ET contact, claimed that his guide hailed from the Jupiter system. His contact explained he flitted between cities on Ganymede and Io, moons of Jupiter. His book *My Contact With Flying*

---

147 www.thelivingmoon.com/47john_lear/02files/Howard_Menger_001.html

Saucers was published in 1959, two years after James reported on his trip to Zomdic.[148]

Kraspedon conducted a lengthy interview with his contact who he refers to as 'The Captain'. This largely reads as science fiction and it may raise eyebrows amongst the world's astrophysicists to learn that there are cities on Jupiter's moons.

Aside from the usual somewhat elusive comments about advanced physics, ministrations against atomic war and imploring for humankind to live harmoniously with nature, The Captain made a series of predictions. He presciently predicted there would be a period of terrorism on Earth. This would become an even more pertinent issue for Kraspedon as he himself was arrested on suspicion of terrorist offences in 1968.[149]

Some other predictions are wider of the mark. For example, The Captain tells Kraspedon that a second sun will enter the solar system, which will either smash the Earth to pieces or attach itself to it. Either way, The Captain warns this will cause the people of Earth to 'have other problems to solve', which is putting it mildly. However The Captain said this catastrophic event would occur by the end of the 20th century, so he has fortunately miscalculated on this point.

Kraspedon describes himself as a Parson and has many questions about the nature of God and God's will. The Captain provides an intriguing definition of 'God',

---

148 *My Contact With Flying Saucers,* Dino Kraspedon, 1959, Spearman

149 *Turn Of Your Mind,* Gary Lachman, 2003, Disinformation Company

explaining 'God is an isotropic line parallel to itself and vibrating on itself at right angles'. He can also be explained by a basic equation, namely 'n = infinity'[150] This doesn't appear to have any meaning as it basically just means that n = n or infinity = infinity.

Much of his writings are complicated musings on magnetism, gravity and the material world. The Captain is dismissive of humankind's physical knowledge and the theory of relativity, remarking that our scientific knowledge is 'very wrong'.

He outlines a cure for cancer saying that instead of taking the usual Earthly approach to cures, sufferers should take an extract of liver with enzymes as these will cause any tumour to recede.

One assessment of Earth that it is hard to disagree with is The Captain's pronouncement that 'Earth is in the hands of raving lunatics'. For all that Kraspedon and his fellow contactees are widely dismissed as fruitcakes, their vision for the organisation of the planet is at least superior to and more desirable than the current system of permaviolence, horror and gross inequality that humankind, its leaders and religions have delivered.

Kraspedon died in 2004.

Another entity from Jupiter, known as 'JW' had contacted American **Gloria Lee** in the early 1950s. Lee was well used to leaving terra firma due to her day job as cabin crew for an American airline.

Lee was a follower of the *Oahspe Bible*, a late 19th century work, supposedly channelled through her fellow countryman, dentist John Ballou Newbrough. Again we

---

150 *My Contact With Flying Sacuers*, ibid

see here spiritualism as a precursor to contacteeism, as Newburgh claimed his work had been produced through automatic writing, a familiar spiritualist trope.

The book also included a number of drawings, which along with the text were said to have been channelled through Newbrough's automatic writings by heavenly angels representing Jehovah. The book outlines a system of grades that beings must gradually attain before they can reach heaven. Heaven is ruled by a high ranking angel who takes charge for a set period of time, somewhat like a president or prime minister would have a fixed term of office.

The notion of all beings going through this process of gradual enlightenment, often based on learning from their immoral acts reminded me in many ways of an early proto-westernised take on Buddhism. All beings are subject to this process, whether they believe in it, an afterlife, anything else or not.[151] The text is grandiose and biblical in tone.

The messages Lee received from JW were reminiscent of those outlined in *The Oahspe* and again we see spiritualist belief being updated to fall in with the shifting gaze of spiritually minded humans from beyond the grave to beyond planet Earth.

Lee made waves in the 1950s contactee scene and released two books, *Why We Are Here!*[152] followed by *The Changing Conditions of Your World*.[153] Both were

---

151 *Oahspe Seven Books of Wisdom,* John Newburgh, Booksurge 2009 (original publication 1892)
152 *Why We Are Here!* Gloria Lee, Cosmon Research Foundation, 1959, Palos Verdes Estates CA
153 *The Changing Conditions of Your World,* Gloria Lee, 1962, Common Research Foundation, 1959, Palos Verdes Estates, CA

teachings from JW. The cover of *Why We Are Here* outlines it is 'written by a being from Jupiter and instrumented by Gloria Lee'.

Sadly her life was to end tragically, one of the mercifully few victims of the contactee's outsider belief system. In 1962, after her plans for world peace fell on deaf ears when taken to the White House, Lee embarked on a protest hunger strike to highlight the crucial issues she had to raise. As a result of complications due to the hunger strike, she died on 2nd December 1962 in George Washington University Hospital. Her hunger strike had lasted over two months.

Ernest Norman dabbled in any number of vocations. Aside from being an electrical engineer by trade, he turned his hand to poetry, science, philosophy and spiritualism while also finding time to engage in channelled communications with 'Martian Ambassador' Nur El.[154] The addition of 'El' as the surname is a little on the nose, 'El' being the surname of Superman's Kryptonian family. Superman himself has the real name of Kal-El. His father is called Jor-El.

Norman's first book, *The Truth About Mars: An Eyewitness Account*,[155] details his meetings with Nur El. Interestingly, unlike James, he is explicit that his journeys to Mars took place while in his astral body. In this form he was able to travel to Mars and around its underground civilisation.

---

154 *Weird California,* Greg Bishop, 2006, Sterling Publishing Company, New York

155 *The Truth About Mars: An Eyewitness Account,* Ernest Norman, 1956, Unarius, El Cajon CA

Norman founded Unarius (Universal Articulate Interdimensional Understanding of Science), an organisation aimed at propagating the messages he had received from Nur El along with Norman's own brand of spiritualism. Rather than going all in on the extraterrestrial hypothesis, Norman, through the Unarius organisation, initially evangelised the Interdimensional Theory. This was the theory developed by among others, Jacques Vallee, which continues today and is more commonly referred to as the Parallel Universes Theory. In this school of thought, the non-human intelligent entities interacting with humankind are not travelling here from actual material planets in nuts and bolts spacecraft. Neither are they the deceased or part of the heavenly and infernal hosts. The Interdimensional Theory postulates that the visitors are in fact from alternate dimensions.

Norman died in December 1971. Sole responsibility for Unarius passed to Norman's wife and co-founder, **Ruth E. Norman**. Ruth Norman would refer to herself as Queen Uriel. Norman was her fourth husband. Despite her solid roots in spiritualism, with her notions of channelling spirits and past life regression techniques, Ruth changed direction and took Unarius increasingly down the road of the Extra-Terrestrial hypothesis as opposed to Interdimensional Theory, following her husband's death.

In 1974 the Unarius Academy purchased land near Jamul, California in order to create a landing site for the 'Space Brothers' that Ruth/Uriel believed were on their way to planet Earth[156]. The mission of the Space Brothers

---

156 *When Prophecy Never Fails: Myth and Reality in a Flying Saucer Group,* Diana Tumminia, 2005, OUP

was to free Earth of all crime and disease, a project set to involve a thousand ET scientists.

The predicted landing did not occur although Ruth/Uriel stoically maintained her belief that she would eventually welcome the Space Brothers. Sadly she was still waiting at the time of her death on 12th July 1993, exactly three weeks before James himself departed on a similar final journey to who knows where, beyond this material world.

Despite the ongoing no show of the Space Brothers, Unarius continues to this day, promoting their messages of spiritual growth and extraterrestrial guidance.[157]

In 1956, the year before James would set off for Zomdic, farmer **Buck Nelson** would release his book *My Trip to Mars, the Moon and Venus*.[158] As with Nelson's contactee contemporaries, the main concern of his new alien friends was humankind's development of nuclear weaponry. Nelson's meeting with the aliens had taken place the year before his book was released, 1955.

Nelson describes that while outside his farmhouse, he saw three flying saucers overhead. Rather than panicking, shouting out a series of expletive variants around the millennial expression 'WTF' and rushing back inside to phone the emergency services, Nelson instead began to take photographs of the craft, while also signalling to them with a torch.

In return they shined a hot beam of light down on him, which he described as being 'much brighter and hotter

---

[157] www.unarius.org
[158] *My Trip to Mars the Moon and Venus*, Buck Nelson, UFOrum Flying Saucer Club, Grand Rapids, 1956

than the sun'. This may sound hostile and potentially life-threatening but in actual fact had the effect of clearing up his lumbago and improving his eyesight. Further to this, three men and a dog, who happened to come from Venus, made contact with him. Almost immediately, they got on Nelson's case about humankind's development of nuclear weaponry.

Once again the question must be asked of the alien visitors as to why they thought the best way of dissuading humankind from their journey down the road to self-inflicted nuclear Armageddon, was to contact a farmer from Missouri. Surely appearing at the White House and curing Eisenhower of his Crohn's disease[159] might have been a more productive opening gambit.

However, it was to Nelson that they pontificated 'we are here to see which way this world will use atomic power, for peace or war. We have stood by and seen other planets, one after another destroy itself. Is this world next? We wonder and wait. Again I say; give up your atomic weapons and may peace be on this Earth'.[160]

They also provided Nelson with 'Twelve Laws of God' which are basically mild re-workings of the biblical ten commandments[161] with a couple of twists. For example 'thou shalt not kill', second of the twelve laws, has now been given the addendum 'includes accidents and war'. Being told by God not to kill people by accident is a curious instruction and one almost impossible to adhere

---

159 Heaton, LD et al, President Eisenhower's Operation for regional enteritis, *Annals of Surgery* 1964
160 *My Trip to Mars, the Moon and Venus* ibid
161 *The Bible*, Exodus 20:1-17

to. A reasonable response would be 'you're God, you stop the accidents' but Nelson doesn't engage in such debate.

There is also intriguing dietary and fashion advice with law 11 stating 'do not drink or eat anything that is not food, wear nothing on the body that harms it or is of no use'.

The story of the initial Ten Commandments sees them given to Moses by a higher intelligence. Perhaps this was the same prescriber of laws who had returned having given them a bit of an update. Nelson died in 1982.

South African contactee **Elizabeth Klarer** was unusual in claiming not only to have had a sexual relationship with an alien being but also to have been blessed by said union, giving birth to an alien-human hybrid child. The alien's name was Akon and he had been in contact with Elizabeth since childhood.

Presumably this contact was telepathic as it wasn't until 7th April 1956 that Akon actually landed his craft, by which time Klarer was aged 46.[162] Similarly to James's journey, Klarer was initially taken to a mothership from whence she was transported to Akon's home planet. This planet was called Meton though, not Zomdic and was in orbit around Alpha Centuri.

It was here that Klarer would deliver Akon's child, who was given the name Ayling. The Hulien (an alien-human hybrid) remained on Meton. It wouldn't be until 1980 that Klarer would publish her book *Beyond the Light Barrier*[163] reporting on her experiences. Klarer died

---

162 *UFOs, Psi and Spiritual Evolution*, Christopher Humphrey, 2005, Adventures Unlimited Press, Kempton IL

163 *Beyond the Light Barrier*, Elizabeth Klarer, 1980, Light Technology Publishing (2008 ed), Flagstaff AZ

of breast cancer in South Africa in 1994, aged 84.[164]

1957, the year of James's experience of travelling to Zomdic was arguably the zenith of the decade in the USA for contactees. Fuelled by Adamski and also Van Tassel's *Giant Rock Interplanetary Space Craft Convention*, the likes of **Wayne Aho**[165] and **Reinhold Schmidt** lectured around California, which was something of a contactee central hub. Aho would also found his own religious group based on his extraterrestrial teachings.

Schmidt's tales were truly fantastical, for example, recounting how he had been taken by 'Mr X', his German-speaking, Saturn-inhabiting alien contact, to the Great Pyramid of Giza, where he was shown a flying saucer that Jesus Christ had used to travel to and from Earth in, from his home planet of Venus.[166] Presumably having left the saucer at some point in the Pyramid, he had hitched a ride back to Venus.

Both Schmidt and particularly Aho, also associated with **Otis Carr** on the contactee lecture circuit. Unusually Carr appears to have been more interested in the craft that the extraterrestrials were using for their intergalactic escapades, rather than their messages surrounding general peace, harmony and the need for nuclear de-escalation.

His company OTC enterprises took inspiration from visionary Nikola Tesla. Carr had patented his own flying

---

164 Sexual Contacts with Aliens Occur Frequently, https://web.archive.org/web/20090203115739/http://english.pravda.ru/science/19/94/378/13623_aliens.html
165 *UFOs & Alien Contact*, Robert Bartholomew & George Howard, 1998, Prometheus Books, New York
166 Reinhold O Schmidt, *The Edge of Tomorrow*, 1975, Inner Light Publications, New Brunswick NJ

saucer prototype and claimed to be working on a version which would be able to travel to and from the Moon in less than a day. His demonstrations of the prototype were however underwhelming, with reports suggesting it would do little more than emit a humming noise.

Carr's vocation as an engineer of extraterrestrial craft and technology would end in ignominy with a conviction in 1961 for fraudulent 'selling of securities'. Unable to pay the $5,000 fine levied, Carr would spend time in jail and disappeared from the contactee scene. He died in Pittsburgh in 1982.[167]

Nuclear stress

One of the key strands running through the DNA of all contactee messages are the instructions that humankind needs to get along with each other and the planet in a peaceful way.

If one were being unkind, it could be pointed out that self-inflicted nuclear Armageddon is self-evidently going to be bad news for humankind and planet Earth. It does not really require an ET to tell people this. There is no real practical advice given on how to deescalate the tensions which existed and persist to this day between the various powerful competing interests on the planet.

Messages seemingly arbitrarily delivered to quite random individuals is unlikely to help much.

There are numerous reports in the Ufological cannon of aliens taking a far more interventionist approach with regard to Earth's nuclear arsenal. Probably the most notable of people to take an interest in the concept of ET interfering in Earth's nuclear affairs was Edgar Mitchell.

---

167 US death index

Mitchell was a NASA astronaut and the sixth person to walk on the moon.

Mitchell was a keen proponent of the ET hypothesis. In 2015, he would tell the Daily Mirror that aliens had kept nuclear military bases under surveillance, when discussing White Sands nuclear testing base. He also said he had spoken with numerous army personnel who had told him that extraterrestrials had appeared frequently around nuclear weapons silos, disabling missiles and even shooting down test missiles.[168]

It is also almost certain that nuclear weapons were held at the US Air Force bases in Rendlesham Forest, Bentwaters and Woodbridge. Rendlesham Forest is second only to Roswell in terms of prominence in ufological circles, with reports from multiple air force personnel of sightings of UFOs over the course of two nights at Christmas 1980. There are many books on the subject of course with the definitive overview provided by Nick Pope[169] who carried out a cold case review while working for the MOD investigating UFOs.

In the book Mr Pope will neither confirm nor deny the presence of nuclear weapons at the base due to the Official Secrets Act he signed and is still bound by. Either this means he doesn't know and is being deliberately mysterious or he knows they are there and can't say. The way he has presented his comments on the matter just about stop short of confirming that nuclear weapons were there, rather than hinting that there weren't any.

---

168 www.mirror.co.uk/news/technology-science/science/peace-loving-aliens-tried-save-6235113
169 *Encounter In Rendlesham Forest,* Nick Pope, 2014

I have stayed overnight in Rendlesham Forest which is an extraordinarily atmospheric place that I would highly recommend. The forest ground is clearly hollow in places, which presumably are the tunnels used to move missiles around underground between the two bases Woodbridge and Bentwaters. In any event, I only mention Rendlesham here as the interest of ET in nuclear weapon bases continued and in fact continues to be a theme in alien contact, sightings and experience.

This could of course be projected human anxiety and deep rooted stress at the possibility of wiping ourselves out in an act of species self-genocide but who really can tell?

It is worth noting that James's warning message for humanity which he brought back from Zomdic relates to use of 'force' generally, rather than specifically in relation to nuclear weapons. However as nuclear weaponry had taken the ramifications for using force to another level of 'Mutually Assured Destruction', it is easy to infer that this would be the main area of concern. As Albert Einstein rather chillingly remarked 'I know not with what weapons World War III will be fought, but World War IV will be fought with sticks and stones'.[170]

I admire the above contactees, groups and followers for at least trying to get across a message of peace to mankind although their contacts do seem short on practical solutions or any real sophistication of method in getting their message across.

As we leave the contactees for now, I would like to present two quotes from people who have travelled in space. In many ways I think they sum up the message

---

170 Interview in *Liberal Judaism* 16, April-May 1949

the contactees were desperate to get across. Namely the protection of planet Earth, a quasi-miraculous unexplained atom of nothing floating through the vast dangerous oceans of space-time.

"You develop an instant state of global consciousness, a people orientation, an intense dissatisfaction with the state of the world and a compunction to do something about it. From out there on the Moon, international politics looks so petty. You want to grab a politician by the scruff of the neck and drag him a quarter of a million miles out and say 'look at that you son of a bitch.'" – Edgar Mitchell, Apollo 14 Astronaut.[171]

"The first day or so we all pointed to our countries. The third or fourth day we were pointing to our continents. By the fifth day we were aware of only one Earth." – Sultan bin Salman Al-Suad, space shuttle astronaut, first Royal and first Muslim in space.[172]

For a fantastic chronology of alien experiencers, I would highly recommend *UFOs and Alien Contact* by Robert Bartholomew and George Howard and particularly table two pages 253-260. The table is very comprehensive with one James Cooke shaped hole being the omission which proves the rule.

---

171 *People Magazine,* 8th April 1974
172 Speech at First Congress of the Association of Space Explorers, Cernay, France, 1985

seven
runcorn window area

> Every science is a mutilated octopus. If its tentacles
> were not clipped to stumps, it would feel its way
> into disturbing contacts.
>
> Charles Fort[173]

Runcorn and its immediate surroundings have had their fair share of UFO activity over the years. The position of an extraordinarily large chemical plant dominating the banks of the Mersey there and pumping any manner of weird and wonderful chemical compounds into the local atmosphere may well have contributed to some of these reports.

Esteemed UFO researcher Jenny Randles coined the evocative phrase 'Wonderland' to refer to the supposed triangular window area for the multitudinous paranormal and ufological activity which has been reported over the years in the locality. The three points of the triangle being the Mersey Estuary at Runcorn, Helsby Hill and Daresbury.[174] Daresbury of course is home to the absolutely charming Lewis Carroll Visitor Centre.[175] Lewis Carroll who was born Charles Lutwidge Dodgson lived in this quiet Cheshire village until he was 11.

---
173 *Wild Talents,* Charles Fort, 1932, Claude Kendall, New York
174 *Paranormal Merseyside,* S.D Tucker ibid
175 www.lewiscarrollcentre.org.uk

I visited the centre, which is inside the village's All Saints Church and would highly recommend dropping in. Numerous characters are captured in the stained glass windows from Carroll's *Alice's Adventure's in Wonderland*, including the Mad Hatter, The March Hare and of course the Cheshire Cat. As a rough guide, think All Saints Church, Daresbury, as one point of the triangle, Helsby Hill where James left for Shelbic as another and the Silver Jubilee Bridge between Runcorn and Widnes as the final point.

There are a number of excellent round-ups online and elsewhere[176] of mysterious activity within this area but I will outline some selected highlights below. My pick of one from each decade.

Runcorn 1963

Slightly hesitant to mention this as I have struggled to trace the provenance of the original source. However it appears to be the most prominent local sighting immediately after James's Zomdic experience. There are multiple mentions online.[177] An RAF veteran named Dick Newby saw a 'huge blue star like object' flying at speed over Boston Avenue in the town. It then burned and blazed a trail over Halton Castle.

Newby allegedly said: "I served for seven years in

---

176 See chapter 'A Window into Wonderland' in *Paranormal Merseyside*, S.D Tucker ibid

177 For example see: https://planetpreternatural.wordpress.com/2011/10/23/a-brief-ufo-history-of-halton-1957-2003/

the RAF and I have heard pilots speak about these flying saucers after returning from operations. I myself was very alarmed. I've seen plenty of shooting stars and airliners but this was neither. It looked nothing like a shooting star and was dead silent."

Frodsham 1978

Frodsham lies immediately south-west of Runcorn, towards Helsby, which is of course where James departed for Shebic.

In 1978, four men sitting next to the River Weaver saw an object like a silver balloon land in a meadow. Mysterious beings emerged, paralysed a cow and put it in a cage. The men sensibly fled, with one reporting later he had some sunburn on his legs and there had been an eerie blue-green glow around the area.[178]

Very hard to call this one. It certainly sounds a tall tale, although hard to establish motive.

The only real conclusion to draw that ticks all the boxes is that a vain, kleptomaniac, entrepreneurial hot air balloon enthusiast decided to get on with some good old fashioned cow rustling. The description of the beings as 'mysterious' doesn't really help of course as landing in a field and paralysing cows is by nature 'mysterious' as opposed to say 'everyday'.

Why is the said entrepreneur vain? Well the witnesses saw a blue-green glow and experienced sunburn. Presumably from some sort of portable sunbed. Too early

---

178 *The UFO Encyclopedia*, John Spencer ibid

for sunbeds you say? Think again! Sunbeds were oranging people up in the late 1970s.[179]

Finally a solution to this mystery.

Runcorn 1981

John and Bell Walsh, along with John's father took a late night walk along the Bridgewater Canal. When approaching a bridge which crossed the canal, they were taken with 'a strange feeling'.

They were comparing how they felt when a bright white light sped towards them and they quickly ran onto the bridge to gain a better view. The light was coming from some laboratories on their left and was moving towards an old water tower, changing back to a brilliant white colour as it did.

The moving object was observed for around 10 minutes and was silent. After it disappeared from view a small plane came from the same direction as the light and in contrast to the bright white object, was very loud.

The Walshes comment they were used to seeing many helicopters and flying craft. The key differential with the white light was the silence.[180] Silent movement was of course also reported by Dick Newby.

Presumably by 'laboratories', the Walshes were referring to Daresbury Laboratory which has a distinctive long stalk mushroom shaped tower. The laboratory began

---

179 www.tanningstudios.co.uk
180 Letter to 'The Unexplained' quoted in *The Mammoth Book of UFOs*, ibid

operations in 1962 and officially opened in 1967 as the Daresbury Nuclear Physics Laboratory.[181]

The Sci-Tech Daresbury campus appears to have its fingers in any number of scientific exploratory pies. Its website notes that: "Daresbury Laboratory is renowned for its world leading scientific research in fields such as computational science, physics, chemistry, materials, *accelerator technology and engineering*."[182] (my italics).

Could they have been carrying out experimentation in aerial craft or drones with silent tech, firing their craft out into the night, then observing the activity from a base in the depths of the campus?

I did email the complex to see if they could advise if any activity, which may explain the Walsh's sighting, had taken place in 1981. They did not respond. Their silence speaks volumes! Maybe.

Project Condign: Runcorn 1996

A Runcorn sighting features in Project Condign, a previously secret UFO study carried out by the Defence Intelligence Staff (DIS) of the UK, commencing in 1997 and running through to 2000.[183]

The report was released into the public domain in 2005 following a Freedom of Information request from notable

---

181 http://www.sci-techdaresbury.com/the-campus/science-facilities/
182 ibid
183 http://webarchive.nationalarchives.gov.uk/20121026065214/
http://www.mod.uk/defenceinternet/freedomofinformation/
publicationscheme/searchpublicationscheme/
unidentifiedaerialphenomenauapintheukairdefenceregion.htm

Fortean writer and lecturer at Sheffield Hallam University Dr David Clarke and Gary Anthony, a former BUFORA (British UFO Research Association) astronomical consultant.

The names of the report's author(s) have not been made public. Its conclusions are interesting but unsurprisingly stop short of concluding that our airspace is being regularly visited by non-human flying craft under intelligent control.

The report does recognise that there are numerous genuine sightings of unexplained aerial phenomenon (UAP) from credible witnesses. However it concludes intriguingly that the phenomenon can largely be attributed to a meteorological plasma manifestation similar in nature to ball lighting. Of course, there are different interpretations of the information and the report is well worth a read.

If nothing else it reveals that the DIS were taking the UFO phenomenon seriously and investigating it in depth until at least relatively recently. No smoking gun of course though, although as we know the smoking gun is locked in a hanger in Area 51, guarded by an army of Sasquatches.[184]

In any event, a Runcorn sighting gets a mention. Not James Cooke however. The unnamed Runcorn resident in question, reported having seen a kite-shaped object at around 5.25am on 25th October 1996. The object had white, green and red lights while flying approximately 250ft in the air. It circled around above the observer for a while before accelerating away at high speed. The observer

---

184 That's my theory anyway, the burden of proof is on you to prove me wrong

advised they had also seen the same craft in November 1994.

Ufological staple Nick Pope passed comment on the matter.[185] Mr Pope was employed by the Ministry of Defence (MOD) between 1985 and 2006 and gained notoriety by being Britain's answer to Fox Mulder from TV's *The X Files*. Between 1991 and 1994 he was tasked with investigating UFO sightings for the MOD.

Mr Pope is quoted as saying 'the Runcorn sighting is certainly a fascinating one and while red, green and white are of course the colours of standard aviation lights, not much is flying at 5.30am and the sudden acceleration is harder to explain in conventional terms'.

Runcorn, The Glen 2009

Someone referred to only as 'Ste' (don't leave a scent for those MIBs to pick up Ste, I like it) was leaving his home at around midnight to drop a friend home when a bright flash lit up the sky like a 'camera flash'. Ste and his friend understandably assumed this was some sort of police helicopter.

He spotted the flash again by Boston Avenue, which is of course where Dick Newby saw his UFO in 1963. Yet again there was no noise. Yet again as with Dick Newby's account, Halton Castle is mentioned. In this instance Halton Castle is where the brightest flash is seen. My favourite line from Ste's statement is, 'took same journey

---

185 http://www.liverpoolecho.co.uk/news/how-runcorn-ufo-sighting-featured-11695712

home, checking the sky as you do in Runcorn'.[186] Indeed you do, indeed you do.

The account is intriguing as this really is correctly to be categorised as an Unidentified Aerial Phenomenon (UAP) rather than UFO. Ste rules out the possibility of it being lightning although this does seem an obvious conclusion to draw. However, he says there was very little cloud cover with stars clearly visible. There were also no accompanying sounds of thunder.

Runcorn, Sandy Lane 2016

An eight-year-old boy reported seeing a classic flying saucer with a dome top on Wednesday September 7th.[187] The sighting took place over Runcorn's energy-from-waste incinerator, with the boy's mother taking a rationalist view, assuming the sighting was of some sort of drone. The drawing the boy did, looks unerringly like the classic George Adamski photograph of a Venusian 'Scout Ship' that Adamski says he snapped at Palomar Gardens, California in December 1952.[188]

Pleasingly this is of course the 59th anniversary of James's trip to Zomdic. Less pleasingly the sighting left the boy extremely shaken up.

---

186 http://www.uk-ufo.co.uk/tag/runcorn/
187 http://www.liverpoolecho.co.uk/news/ufo-reported-shining-green-beams-11863707
188 *Flying Saucers Have Landed,* D Leslie & G Adamski ibid

Conclusions

There are hundreds of sightings of UFOs over Runcorn, a town with a population of around 61,000. I will be clear and say that I don't know if this is standard when compared to towns of similar size but it does seem to be something that has become meshed with the feel of the place. For example, the comment about watching the skies in the 2009 account is accurate. Local people are aware of it as a place where the unusual happens or at least is said to happen.

There could of course be very material reasons for this. The town has long been associated with the chemical industry. When I was growing up during the Cold War, there was what may have been merely a local urban myth that it was one of the top targets for the Soviets in the event of nuclear war. The reason? Because not only would the nuke wreak havoc with the industrial North West of England, but the added value of the chemical plants going up would wipe out much of the Midlands too and further north due to damage from the chemicals blowin' in the wind.

To this day chemical giant Ineos has a huge plant there[189] among others.

So the chemicals are polluting people's minds and making them see things right? No, that is absolutely not my conclusion, particularly if any of these multinational fume-makers are feeling litigious.

What I think more likely is that chemicals, safely my global-industrial-chemical friends of course, being

---

189 http://www.ineos.com/businesses/ineos-enterprises/sites/

released into the atmosphere, combine with the elements already present there, to produce the orange balls, flashes and lights. It is this chemical atmospheric interaction which accounts for many of the other UAPs and UFOs which are reported. Pareidolia probably aids and abets also when the local populace view such UAP activity.

EIGHT
JAMES COOKE SPIRITUALIST

> Is there anybody there?
> Unattributed

So one thing that has been established is that James was a spiritualist and a key component of a group known as The Aquarian Crusades.

This positions James in the prototype New Age movement, even before he met his new friends from Zomdic, 'beyond the spirit world'.

The concept of the 'Age of Aquarius' has of course commonly been adopted by what we would now refer to as 'New Age' groups. It refers to the astrological movement of the Earth from the constellation of Pisces to the constellation of Aquarius. This was hoped by many to be the dawning of a new more peaceable age for humankind.

The cycle of the precession of the equinoxes sees the position of the sun at the time of the March (vernal) equinox move into a new constellation. This cycle through the 12 astrological ruling signs, occurs approximately every 2150 years.[190]

The astrological concept of the new dawning age received some oxygen in the 1920s, with books such as

---

190 http://earthsky.org/human-world/when-will-the-age-of-aquarius-begin

The Message of Aquaria[191] and *The Riddle of the Aquarian Age*[192] being released in this decade. Daily newspapers in Britain were also referencing the concept in the 1930s.[193] However, there appears to be little record of the concept in the media or literature throughout the 1940s and 1950s. Possibly the horror of the second world war mitigated against too much navel gazing regarding the potential effect on humanity of astronomical passage.

The resurgence of Aquarius as a totem of unconventional religion and spiritualism does not undergo a resurgence until the 1960s[194], so The Aquarian Crusades were certainly ahead of the curve with their choice of name.

The Encyclopaedia Britannica, places the 'New Age' movement as something that spread through non-mainstream religions in the 1970s and 1980s[195] so again it is revealed that James was surfing the front of the wave when it came to updating spiritualism to contactee and new age thought.

British Spiritualism experienced something of a renaissance following the world wars which dominated the start of the 20th century. Understandable given the unimaginable ubiquitous grief, senseless loss of life and brutality.

At the start of the 1930s it was estimated that there were around a quarter of a million people in the UK who

---

191 *The Message of Aquaria: The Significance & Mission of the Aquarian Age,* F & H Curtiss, 1921, Washington
192 *The Riddle of the Aquarian Age,* Julius Bennett, 1925, London
193 *Children of the New Age: A History of Spiritual Practices,* S Sutcliffe, 2003, Routledge, New York
194 *Children of the New Age,* Ibid
195 www.britannica.com/topic/New-Age-movement

identified themselves as spiritualists, with approximately 2,000 spiritualist societies and any number of home groups in operation.[196] The Aquarian Crusades would have fallen into the home group category with James its de facto leader and chief medium.

During the First World War, Runcorn Spiritualist Church offered hospitality and recuperation to wounded soldiers.[197]

In the 1950s there were actually two dominant denominations of Spiritualism in Britain. The Spiritualists National Union (SNU) positioned itself as a wholly separate religion whereas the Christian Spiritualist Movement (CSM) saw itself as compatible with and a part of Christianity.[198]

It is hard to say exactly where the Aquarian Crusades group stood in terms of the Spiritualist dichotomy but it appears it was going its own way. There is no mention of Christianity in James's interviews. Spiritualism was not naturally aligned with the concept of alien contacteeism either. James is folding alien contactee philosophy into the basic spiritualist mixture and creating what would present a couple of decades later as a 'New Age' church.

The lack of Christianity being mentioned by James notwithstanding, it should be borne in mind that *The Aquarian Gospel of Jesus the Christ* by Levi H. Dowling had been released in 1908.[199]

---

196 *Children of the New Age,* ibid, page 36
197 http://www.runcorn-snu.org.uk/history/
198 www.ibuzzle.com/articles/the-spiritualist-church-and-the-role-of-mediums.html
199 Levi H Dowling, *The Aquarian Gospel of Jesus the Christ*, 1908, ES Dowling Publisher, Los Angeles CA

The Aquarian Gospel of Jesus the Christ basically covers the two-decade 'gap year' that Jesus took in the canonical gospels between birth and beginning his ministry in Galilee.[200] During this time, according to the gospel, he pre-empted the hippiedom of the 1960s by some 1,980 years, hitting Tibet, Greece and India.

The *Aquarian Gospel* would become a staple of hippy alternative literature in the 1960s. There is a good chance that The Aquarian Crusades had taken its motif from the book which has a much more esoteric and spiritualist vibe to it than the traditional bibilical New Testament.

Contact with spirits via mediums had been popular in the second half of the 19th century, with séances, Ouija boards, ectoplasm and the like providing entertainment and intrigue to the inhabitants of Victorian Britain. There were notable ongoing debates about the veracity of such phenomena or otherwise, not least between such luminaries as Sir Arthur Conan Doyle who was convinced by the phenomenon and Houdini, who wasn't.

Many mediums were exposed under the scrutiny of investigators, having been shown to be using the tricks of stage magicians to manifest supposed otherworldly phenomenon.

The Society for Psychical Research, founded in 1882, was particularly rigorous in investigating mediums as well as other ghostly phenomenon. Despite the exposure of various mediums, belief in the phenomenon still remained and was largely a question of faith. For example, The Bangs Sisters were two mediums who operated out of Chicago in

---

[200] Book of Matthew, *The Bible* 4:12-25 by someone called Matthew presumably but disputed

the late 19th century. They produced spirit portraits and although magicians have proposed theories as to how they may have been able to do this, this does not necessarily mean that the sisters themselves were using such trickery. Just because a magician can replicate a supposed psychic phenomenon does not mean that the phenomenon is therefore definitively a trick.

There are numerous intersecting points between spiritualist practices. What does appear clear is that James was anxious to update his more traditional spiritualist roots. Where before the contact was with spirit guides and the dearly departed, he would now add alien beings into the mix.

Indeed the method of contacting both aliens and spirits appears to have been broadly the same, James's actual trip to Zomdic notwithstanding. Members of the Church of Aquarius are reported to have sat around a glowing plate in a dark room, a practice which enabled them to receive their visions.[201] This type of practice in fact dated back centuries. Michel De Nostredame, aka Nostramus, would stare into a bowl of water positioned on top of a tripod. Doing this for long periods of time would produce visions and prophecies. There is also an indication that he may have stared through a candle flame at the water to further enhance its hallucinatory qualities although some historians have interpreted Nostradamus's notes about using a 'flame' as referring to the flame of inspiration as opposed to an actual fiery light.[202]

---

201 *Flying Saucerers,* ibid, page 95

202 *Nostradamus For Dummies*, Scarlett Ross, 2005, Wiley and Sons, Hoboken NJ

Cha-chu-ka

James of course also had a spirit guide named Cha-chu-ka. Often, particularly in America, guides would be associated with Native Americans. Cha-chu-ka would certainly be an exotic sounding name for a furniture salesman-cum-greengrocery manager from Runcorn in the 1950s.

Cha-chu-ka is actually a Swahili word, referencing various movements of the sea, namely 'heave', 'roll' and 'surge'. It is also the Swahili word for 'ferment'.

Anyone who grew up in Runcorn in the 1980s and 1990s will be familiar with a strange piece of enigmatic graffiti emboldened on a brick wall in the Old Town, stating boldly 'Roy speaks Swahili!' Different in tone to the usual 'LFC this or that', 'such and such is a grass', 'free the weed' etc that would often adorn various walls around the town. Perhaps Cha-chu-ka was still on the go and had been in touch again with another Runcorn inhabitant.

The more likely explanation is the one I was given, which was that Roy was a taxi dispatch operator who worked for a local taxi firm. Although a popular employee the local cabbies would often complain that they couldn't understand a word he said, with one of them immortalising (well not quite), Roy's foible in graffiti form.

Band Fluterscooter had a track on their self-titled 2007 album called 'Cha-chuka-ka' so perhaps they are now channelling this particular being, but then again perhaps not.

An internet image search for Cha-chu-ka brings up pictures of a dish, appearing to consist of fried eggs on a bed of what appear to be fried peppers, tomatoes and the like. Mexican, I would say. Not particularly helpful when trying to get a handle on whether Cha-chu-ka has any meaning beyond simply being an exotically impressive sounding nom de plume for a spirit guide.

James with his spirit guide, house-based spiritualist church group, automatic writing, trance states, references to Aquarius and spirit worlds fitted comfortably into the 1950s spiritualist scene.

These were his religious roots. He was not an arriviste by the time flying saucers and science fiction were tightening their unearthly grips on a jittery populace. James was well versed with dealing with other-earthly powers and moved seamlessly to link the spiritual and the extraterrestrial.

James Cooke to Zomdic and beyond

What then, to make of James's tale. A tale that has permeated the Ufological canon and mythos.

Unfortunately, it appears that Zomdic does not exist. At least not in any material sense. However, having considered all the literature, James's own accounts and the social context within which he was operating, a picture does begin to emerge of what might have happened.

Two things can be laid to rest. James was not an alien abductee. The general notion that he was Britain's first alien abductee is sadly misattributed. Neither is he Britain's first alien contactee, with George King having beaten him to the punch.

However, he is a compelling figure.

James, as we have seen had his roots in spiritualism. There is nothing to indicate that he was not devout in his beliefs in higher powers. Initially his focus had been on the spiritual, with guidance coming from beings of the spirit realm such as Cha-chu-ka.

As had been the case in the US, within the context of the growing societal fixation on flying saucers and alien beings, many channelers and spiritualists would turn their attention to contacting alien beings. Often the means of communication were, and continue to be, markedly similar to those utilised to contact the spirit world; trance states, channelling, automatic writing and the like. James himself would use these methods and was introduced to the Zomdickians by his spirit guide Cha-chu-ka. The two worlds of spiritualism and contacteeism were happy bedfellows, ironically in marked contrast to the slightly fractious relationship that can exist between ufologists and mediums.

Both Michael Dale of the *Sunday People* and Thelma Roberts of *Flying Saucer Review* find him convinced of his beliefs. Dale clearly had an agenda to expose what he saw as a crackpot cult, taking funds from a public who did not realise exactly what they were donating to. However, he still concludes that James was convinced of his own beliefs, including the fact that he had travelled to Zomdic in a flying saucer.

James and the wider contactee movement in general, were also reacting to the new unwelcome prospect for humanity of nuclear Armageddon. The need for humankind to sort out their differences was an urgent message that needed to be delivered and who better to deliver it than technologically superior beings who had often witnessed first-hand the damage that nuclear war could wreak?

James was devout and committed to his cause. His ongoing roles as furniture salesman and grocery manager, show that he wasn't made rich by his escapades and stories. For me, it is too cynical a stretch to conclude he was simply a failed con-artist. People found him likeable and charismatic but also that he was convinced of his spiritual beliefs and accompanying fantastical claims.

In studying and reflecting on paranormal phenomenon, there are two key initial questions, namely: 1) Is the person reporting the phenomenon lying? 2) If they are not lying, what is the nature of the phenomenon?

With question 1, I actually think the answer is nuanced and leads to the answer to question 2. No, I do not think James was lying, hoaxing or misrepresenting. This of course is a judgement call and based on the balance of probability. James was devoutly committed to his brand of spiritualism/contacteeism for many years. This brought him little by way of profitability. He was no Erik von Daniken or David Icke, able to generate a well-heeled lifestyle based on his output. Before any Danikenians or Ickeians take issue with this comparison, I am not accusing them of being insincere in their beliefs either. I am just making the point that in the case of James, we can rule out financial incentive as his motivation.

I believe that James believed his tales. This was also the considered opinion of reporters who met him. This does not indicate that he was in contact with a spirit guide called Cha-chu-ka or travelled to an alien world with flying musical cars. However, having weighed up all I know about James, his stories, reports of his character, his professional life, the context of the time he lived in and what I know about humans, my answer to the posed question of 'was he lying?' is no.

So, this leads us to question 2 – What is the nature of the phenomenon? I believe it links in to what in the area of mainstream religion would be called 'faith'.

If nothing else, James clearly had a vivid imagination. By this I don't mean simply the ability to create tall tales, I mean he possessed the ability through the force of will found in his creative personality to convince himself that there was more to the world than the materially observable. This initially came in the form of his attachment to spiritualism and its subsequent weaving into space age contacteeism.

For me there is really no difference in James's beliefs in spirit guides and Zomdickians than there is in mainstream religious beliefs into inscrutable and unobservable deities with seemingly capricious interests in the affairs of humankind; with their generally unheeded messages of peace and harmony. For me, these wishes come from somewhere deep in the collective psyche of humankind, rather than an otherworld per se.

I have no doubt James embellished and stretched his tales. His subsequent tale of a journey to Shebic seems particularly ill conceived. Does this mean his entire output was just a lie? I would say not. My interpretation is that James, fuelled by his strong beliefs in the spirit world and higher compassionate intelligences, coupled with his creative mind's eye had convinced himself that the foundation of his tales were true and he was a conduit for such messages. James would have been able to justify playing fast and loose with the detail to himself, as necessary in getting the crucial message across to his fellow humans, who lacking his spiritual attunement, were not able to experience first-hand contact with these otherworldly intelligences.

A similar process can be observed in many people of 'faith'.

For my own part, having attempted to put myself into the mind-set of a 1950s contactee, I can attest that due almost certainly to auto-suggestion, things that probably aren't particularly significant can leap out and whisper persuasively into one's ear that they are indicators of the 'other'.

For example, the synchronicity between calling a chapter *A Night to Remember* and the box that the *Sunday People* containing the article about James from 1966 came in, saying *Day to Remember*, on the same day that the landline rang in the early hours of the morning – the only time this had happened – seemed peculiar and significant. Almost as though there was a presence on my shoulder. Maybe James? I had felt compelled to write up his tale.

Then add into the mix the eerie coincidence of the random search for word cards, bringing up a company whose website had the cards arranged in to the sentence 'look up into the sky to see me'. Then the exact page of the bible with the Serpent, talking to Eve having vanished. What was all of this? What if anything did it mean? Was it James's way of indicating he didn't want to be associated in any way with said adversary?

Well, almost certainly no, on all counts. Coincidences and nothing more. Random and arguably silly occurrences, just a tale told by an idiot, full of sound and fury, signifying nothing. As someone once said.

But, it was persuasive, tempting, and seductive. Maybe there are higher intelligences, maybe they did contact these seemingly random individuals in the 1950s, who lacking in any political influence were driven to produce their literature and evangelise a message of peace.

In any event. I can well imagine James, being committed to his spiritual beliefs and deep conviction to make the world a better place, somehow convincing himself that his experiences were in some sense real.

There was more, whenever I sat at the table writing about James, I kept noticing flashes out of the corner of my eye. Thinking they may be cars going past on a nearby window, I readjusted my position but the flashes continued. I had never noticed them when seated in that position before. Was this Cha-chu-ka? Was it the Zomdickians signalling to me from beyond the spirit world? Again, no. Immersing myself in and reading swathes of 1950s contactee literature had taken its toll. But I felt the pull. The lure of being a part of something esoteric and important.

Intrigued, I contacted a couple of psychics to see if they would be willing to set up a session in an attempt to contact the Zomdickians or Cha-chu-ka. Being arguably spiritual beings, I wanted to at least attempt to re-establish contact. I received two encouraging responses from local psychics but both went to ground before coming through with an actual contactee session. The search continues and attempted contact with Zomdic will be made at some point.

I understood the reticence of the psychics, I had said I was looking for a good sport and had been transparent about wanting to include the channelling session in a book. One actually said they would probably be setting themselves up for a fall. I respected their decision, although was disappointed at being thwarted. Still, maybe contact with Zomdic and Cha-chu-ka is something I have to pursue myself, to prove my commitment to said beings. Maybe not though. In fact almost definitely not.

So where is the contactee movement today?

A work colleague of mine, who once went by the nickname 'Carpet' and myself, had been discussing a recent podcast episode of The Unexplained, presented by veteran radio broadcaster and podcaster Howard Hughes.[203] In this particular episode, American Randy Kramer was making a number of claims regarding his status as a member of an intergalactic defence force, tasked with protecting planet Earth from various nefarious alien influences. Kramer also mentioned a colleague of his, also from planet Earth, who was employed by the intergalactic force. His name is Corey Goode.

Carpet had forwarded me a YouTube interview between Corey Goode and David Wilcock.[204]

Goode discussed shape-changing aliens the 'Blue Avians', claiming they had visited Earth for a number of years. He referenced the 1950s contactees and was

---

[203] www.theunexplained.tv, Edition 295 – Captain Randy Kramer & Nick Pope, 11 May 2017

[204] Cosmic Disclosure with David Wilcock / Corey Goode, YouTube

comfortable outlining how they had been visited by extraterrestrials, delivering the anti-nuclear weapon message that as we have seen was a major strand of the 1950s contactee movement.

Goode claims to have met the Blue Avians, who communicated with him telepathically, telling him to get rid of his negativity. The message the Blue Avians had for mankind was that humanity needs to become 'more loving… more forgiving of yourself and others and they say that this stops the wheel of karma and we should focus on becoming service to others on a daily basis… raise our consciousness and our vibration'.

This could have come straight out of 1950s contactee literature. It certainly sounds persuasive but I would argue is typically lacking in any practical advice on how to achieve such a state. Goode says the Blue Avians were adamant he and they should not become the focus of a cult or religion, as had happened when they had attempted human contact in the past. Perhaps James Cooke was one of the people they had previously made contact with.

The contactee concept of alien beings, who possess higher intelligence, both moral and technological, still percolates around in society without ever quite taking hold as a mainstream embedded branch of religion, merging spiritualism with extraterrestrial contact, as James Cooke had hoped to achieve.

The nuclear threat has not gone away. North Korea have now developed inter-continental nuclear weaponry and there is no reason to expect that proliferation will be curtailed. Although contentious in some quarters there is large consensus that climate change is the major threat to the continued existence of planet Earth as a living place for intelligent life forms.

In terms of religions, The Aetherius Society founded by George King still offers an organisation for the dispersal of the teachings garnered from extraterrestrial intelligence.

However, for all of the many supernatural belief systems and religions on planet Earth, the various gods and perceived higher intelligences still fail to intervene to any noticeable effect, they remain absent. Taking an agnostic position, this may be simply that such beings don't exist although of course absence of evidence cannot simply be assumed to be evidence of absence. At the very least we are the universe reflecting on itself. This reflection leads to many different conclusions and down many wild and wonderful paths.

It has been an interesting journey with James Cooke and the 1950s contactees. Whatever happened with them, the central messages of love peace and the brotherhood of man were nothing new. Such messages had been present in the major historical world religions for many centuries.

The contactee message is updated for the space age, with angels replaced with ETs and care for the existence of planet Earth added as a post-modern religious strand, harking back to ancient cultural traditions of nature worship. The traditional religions largely explored and provided rules on how humanity should interact and behave on a micro level. With the advent of the nuclear age and the prospect of human-induced Armageddon and environmental catastrophe, the message of the aliens via their contactee missionaries took a more macro view, preaching that humans needed to come together to save the planet and humanity as a whole.

Like the traditional religions, such teachings were ascribed to higher intelligences but in light of the continued absence of any direct contact from these alien and spiritual intelligences, contact that would be simple in this age of mass media, it seems likely that these are and have always been human concerns being ascribed to higher intelligences, in the hope that people will listen and the world will someday fulfil its potential as a beautiful idyll, rather than the fractious, war ravaged, polluted and belligerent place that we know and love.

It is certainly hard to blame James for wanting that.

BIBLIOGRAPHY

Adams, Douglas, *The Hitchhiker's Guide to the Galaxy*, 1979, Pan Books, Basingstoke

Adamski, George & Leslie, Desmond, *Flying Saucers Have Landed*, 1953, T Werner Laurie, London

Angelucci, Orfeo (ed. Palmer, Ray), *The Secret of the Saucers*, 1955, Amherst Press, Wisconsin

Asimov, Isaac, *Second Foundation*, 1953, Gnome Press, New York City

Bartholomew, Robert & Howard, George *UFOs & Alien Contact*, 1998, Prometheus Books, New York

Bennet, Julius, *The Riddle of the Aquarian Age*, 1925, Kessinger, London

Bishop, Greg, *Weird California*, 2006, Sterling Publishing Company, New York

Clarke, Arthur C, *The City and the Stars*, 1956, Frederick Muller Ltd, London

Clarke, David & Roberts, Andy, *Flying Saucerers*, 2007, Alternative Albion, Loughborough

Curtiss, Harriette & Curtiss, F, *The Message of Aquaria*, 1921, The Curtiss Philosophic Book Co, Washington

Dowling, Levi H, *The Aquarian Gospel of Jesus the Christ*, 1908, ES Dowling Publisher, Los Angeles CA

Fort, Charles, *Wild Talents*, 1932, Claude Kendall, New York

Fry, Daniel, *The White Sands Incident*, 1954, New Age – my edition 1992, Horus House Press, Wisconsin

Hancock, Graham, *Fingerprints of the Gods*, 1995, Reed, London

Heinlein, Robert, *Citizen of the Galaxy*, 1957, Scribners, New York City

Hough, Peter & Randles, Jenny, *Mysteries of the Mersey Valley*, 1993, Sigma Leisure, Wilmslow

Humphrey, Christopher, *UFOs, Psi and Spiritual Evolution*, 2005, Adventures Unlimited Press, Kempton IL

Icke, David, *In The Light of Experience*, 1993, Time Warner, New York City

Jung, Carl, *Flying Saucers*, 1978, Princeton, New Jersey

Jung, Carl, *Memories Dreams Reflections*, 1963, Collins and Routledge & Keegan Paul, Abingdon

Keel, John, *UFOs Operation Trojan Horse*, 1971, Souvenir Press, London

Keel, John, *Visitors From Space: The Astonishing True Story of the Mothman Prophecies*, 1975, Panther Books, London

Klarer, Elizabeth, *Beyond the Light Barrier*, 1980, Light Technology Company, Flagstaff AZ

Kraspedon, Dino *My Contact With Flying Saucers*, 1959, Spearman, Jersey

Lachman, Gary, *Turn off Your Mind*, 2003, Disinformation Company, New York City

Lee, Gloria, *The Changing Conditions of Your World*, 1962, Common Research Foundation, Palos Verdes Estates CA

Lee, Gloria, *Why We Are Here!*, 1959, Common Research Foundation, Palos Verdes Estates CA

Menger, Howard, *From Outer Space to You*, 1959, Saucerian, Clarksburg VA

Nelson, Buck, *My Trip to Mars, the Moon and Venus*, 1956, UFOrum Flying Saucer Club, Grand Rapids

Newbrough, John, *Oahspe Seven Books of Wisdom*, 1892, Oahspe Publishing, New York

Norman, Ernest, *The Truth About Mars*, 1956, Unarius, El Cajon CA

Picknett, Lynn, *The Mammoth Book of UFOs*, 2001, Constable, London

Pilkington, Mark, *Mirage Men*, 2010, Constable, London

Pope, Nick, *Encounter in Rendlesham Forest*, 2014, Thistle, London

Ross, Scarlett, *Nostradamus For Dummies*, 2005, Wiley & Sons, Hoboken NJ

Schmidt, Reinhold, *The Edge of Tomorrow*, 1975, Inner Light Publications, New Brunswick NJ

Shakespeare, William, *The Tragedy of Hamlet Prince of Denmark*, circa 1599-1602

Spencer, John, *The UFO Encyclopedia*, 1991, Headline, London

Sutcliffe, Steven J, *Children of the New Age*, 2003, Routledge, London

Swift, Jonathan, *Gulliver's Travels*, 1726, Benjamin Motte, London

Thompson, Dave, *The Changing Face of Runcorn*, 2004, Sutton, Stroud

Tucker, SD, *Paranormal Merseyside*, 2013, Amberley Publishing, Stroud

Tumminia, Diana, *When Prophecy Never Fails*, 2005, OUP, Oxford

Van Tassel, George W, *I Rode in a Flying Saucer*, 1952, New Age Publishing Co, Los Angeles

Van Tassel, Georg W, *Into this World and out Again*, 1956, The College of Universal Wisdom, Yucca Valley California

Van Tassel, George W, *Proceedings of the College of Universal Wisdom*, 1969, Yucca Valley California

Van Tassel, George W, *When Stars Look Down*, 1976, The Krukeberg Press, Los Angeles

Verne, Jules, *Around the World in Eighty Days*, 1873, Dean & Son, London

Von Daniken, Erich, *Chariots of the Gods*, 1968, Putnam, New York City

Wells, II G, *The War of the Worlds*, 1898, William Heinemann, London

Wilde, Oscar, *The Picture of Dorian Gray*, 1890, Lippincott's Monthly Magazine, Philadelphia

Thanks and Acknowledgments

Firstly I'd like to thank my brother Olie Clay for his assistance with editing, reading, cover work and traipsing round Runcorn Hill, treading in the footsteps of James.

I'd like to thank my wife Jenny for agreeing to this book being produced rather than a set of French doors.

Along with Olie, I'd like to thank brother Ben and sister Rachel (my brother and sister, not a monk and a nun) for Rendlesham and the many other Fortean trips and trails we've followed.

Also thanks to Halton Library, Runcorn for the microfiche enabling and artist Chiz for his excellent pop-up UFO installation.

Final thanks to the people of Runcorn. Who loves ya?!